FIRST EDITION
ISBN 978-0-9952885-5-3

1. Supernatural Suspense 2. Haunted House
3. Psychological Horror 4. Ghost Story
5. Crime Fiction 6. Cold Case 7. Paranormal
Thriller

Michael Poeltl

For my Auntie, Andi

Michael Poeltl

Chapter 1 - Jesse

I've always been good at being invisible. Forgettable. Indistinguishable from the wallpaper. I often feel like I'm simply haunting the world I inhabit. An enigma both to the world and myself. It's cringeworthy to be me, and although I'm well into my final year of university, my lack of interest in societal norms remains unchanged. However, a new development is looming. Something dangerous - something tangible I can cling to. Something to solve. But, at what cost?

As a youth, I was diagnosed with selective mutism —a side effect, they said, of my first four years of silence. As a result, I became unusually observant of others. I learned about the world through observation rather than engagement, and by studying how people carried themselves, whether their shoulders sank after an insult or their chests puffed out like proud roosters when receiving a compliment. Conveying their emotions without making a sound. I also noticed how expressions changed, even subtly, such as a raised eyebrow or a slight flinch, to convey mood, and how insecurities crept into conversation. When I finally decided to speak, and I'm not entirely sure it was a decision rather than an impulse that overtook me, my vocabulary surprised my bourgeois parents. They cried together as I watched their newfound pride wash the despair from their eyes. I had compiled a dictionary's worth of words at four and a half and presented them in short, brilliant stanzas. Or so they told their friends. Saying, 'I told you so,' and 'I said it wouldn't last forever.'

Not long after this milestone was reached, I would learn that my sudden, overwhelming need to talk did not lend itself to making friends. It was as if I spoke a different language from the other Kindergarteners. They shied away from my big words and left me alone. I felt like an alien amongst them. Alienated. That's when I decided to halt the progress my parents saw in me and stop talking. To become invisible. Forgettable. At one with the wallpaper.

Since then, I've felt invisible for most of my life. My mother loved me, while my father tolerated me. My father never understood why I might stop speaking. Was it something he'd done? Something he'd said? It wasn't. But the breakthrough they'd witnessed had abruptly ceased, and Dad was visibly upset over it. "I have nothing to say," I would insist.

"But people want to hear from you, Jesse. Your opinions matter," my mother would intercede.

"I don't have opinions," I would rebut.

Of course, that wasn't true. I did have opinions. My head swam with them. Analyzing how others spoke and what they spoke about. Gossip bored me. In my view, it was the lowest common denominator in human relations.

Why talk about someone else when you could avoid it altogether?

And I avoided it, like the plague. I wouldn't answer the other kids if they asked me about another student. I refused to participate in the unqualified assumptions of the other eight-year-olds who thought Micky liked Jules or presumed that Jane was from a house with two mothers and Jackson never washed his hair. Ugg, so *tedious* and unnecessary! It wasn't worth opening my mouth to prove them wrong. It was barely worth a shrug.

Of course, this kind of disinterest in what the kids were saying further distanced me from them. Eventually, they stopped sharing their misguided assumptions with me and started talking about me.

"Jesse is weird," some said. "Jesse can't talk, he can't hear, he's stupid, Jesse is retarded, he isn't even human." Well, they could say whatever they wanted. It was merely erroneous gossip with no basis in fact. Still, I wasn't without feelings, and I cried myself to sleep countless times over the cruel opinions of my peers, even if I was the cause of it.

So, I became more callous. Locking my feelings away, I conducted experiments on my peers to avoid feeling utterly disconnected from the world. My earliest memory of intentionally interrupting the norm was pinching a girl in grade 3 and slipping between two classmates, making her believe one of them had pinched her. They were both oblivious to my cunning, and the girl, Allanah, glared at them angrily. The boys looked at one another and shrugged.

It was so easy to manipulate people, I thought, as I enjoyed a private laugh at my classmate's expense. My mother would later describe the sensation as butterflies in my tummy because the prank was so agreeable. In fact, I liked the sensation so much that I repeated this disturbance several times that afternoon. Soon, the girls were talking in tight groups, gossiping about which boy had been pinching them. They were all wrong.

The feelings that followed were complicated, as I felt clever for evading their suspicions but invisible because they hadn't even considered me the villain. It was as if I had become a ghost.

So, invisible became my norm. Throughout my student career, I remained mute to most. My report cards repeated the same commentaries: *'Jesse is encouraged to seek teacher feedback. Jesse is withdrawn. Jesse is quiet and shy. Jesse should strive to establish connections with his classmates. Jesse should join a club.'*

High school proved relentless, as it does for anyone lacking the necessary social skills. When I was asked to join the D&D Club—a group one might think would appeal to someone with such an aversion to every other organized club—I shook my head and walked away. It wasn't that I felt superior; instead, I felt so detached that the idea of spending endless hours battling mythical creatures in a sparsely furnished, unfinished basement filled with the smell of body odour, soda, and Cheetos alongside my peers made no sense—intellectually. I knew how this sounded, but it was not something I could control.

Disconnected. That's how I felt about the world. It made sense. I didn't question why I felt this way. I wasn't making any effort to be connected, as most people did, so why would I feel any different? It didn't bother me. I no longer went home and cried over the cruelty of others. I didn't feel anything about it. It was what it was.

I was bullied from time to time, but my lack of reaction offered little satisfaction to those performing the bullying. Without a whimper or an attempt to fight back, bullies received no dopamine and so became less interested. My life became increasingly programmed around conducting my experiments as I attended every school dance, every award ceremony in the gym, and every social event alone. My trials in these social situations brought back the butterflies I'd become dependent on. Everyone I'd gleaned a reaction from breathed new life into me. My private joke.

Something as simple as a dead stare from the corner of the gymnasium during a dance when a couple was engaged in a kiss paid dividends to my sensory bank once they realized my attention was directed at them. In one scenario, a boy named Richard approached me after his girlfriend, Diana, noticed that I was noticing them.

"Can I help you?" Richard snarled, his face just inches away. We both stood six feet tall and could see into one another's eyes. Richard was a member of several sports teams, and by all accounts, he enjoyed the life afforded him by participating in those elite social clubs.

I, of course, said nothing in reply. Even if I'd wanted to, and I didn't, I couldn't have responded. I met

Richard's stare without emotion, without a trace of expression.

"Maybe you should leave," the Jock scoffed, but I was frozen in place. Being found out was my drug. It's what gave me all the feels. I wasn't going anywhere.

Richard, becoming enraged by my lack of reaction, shoved me. Although I'm no athlete, I barely budged at the two-handed push. I was no slouch. I rivalled Richard's athletic frame, weighing 200 pounds in my senior year. In addition to the zero response to his suggestion that I leave, this refusal to budge further amplified Richard's anger. He stepped back to size me up.

I felt the impact of Richard's fist slam into my broad jaw, head snapping to the side. The sensation was new, but admittedly not unsolicited. I was no stranger to pain. I had been cutting since I was nine. I had been pinching and punching and slapping myself for years to petition feelings. Oddly, none had produced an emotional reaction in the mirror where I'd stand, applying the techniques and waiting for an expression other than my trademark deadpan to play out across my pale face.

Richard was quickly sequestered by a teacher who was supervising the dance. The teacher, Mr. Duncan, who stood four inches taller than us, was the coach for several of the senior sports clubs. He put himself between me and Richard, turning to Richard.

"Be *better* than this, Rich; you don't need to be hitting the *freak* and missing games." Duncan glared at me over his shoulder. "Go home," he told me.

Instead of soliciting more feelings by ignoring Mr. Duncan, I read the urgency in the man's eyes, straightened my head, turned, and left.

That same night, I reconsidered my approach to people. Could I evoke other emotions in them rather than continually feeding off the dark side? What if I were to make people laugh? Not *at* me, but *with* me. People laughed at me in the halls and behind my back, but that snickering also indulged the dark side. Laughing at someone is as cruel as physically striking them, in my opinion. There is no joy there, only violence.

Upon returning home, I stood before my mirror and devised a joke based on observations I'd made listening to my parents bicker and from television shows. My upturned desk lamp cast a yellow light over the room, creating shadows across my face that hinted at a smile. Imagine dropping your drink on someone's white shirt, filled with grape juice or red wine. That's not funny in itself, but it would leave an untreatable stain and ruin that person's shirt. Make it the wife. They never forget an offence. Make it an accident. They can be funny. Okay, I was ready. Butterflies: standing by.

In my deadpan tone, I delivered the joke aloud, hating the sound of my voice. "So, a husband and wife are at an outdoor concert enjoying the music of a favourite artist when a small plane crashes a hundred yards from the venue. The shock of this sudden event causes the husband to jerk, forcing the red wine in his plastic cup to spill onto his wife's white top.

"The husband turns to meet her scowl. He knows he's fucked up. He knows she'll bring up the time he spilled his drink and ruined her white top at that concert, while conveniently ignoring the plane crashing into the parking lot. She has twenty identical tops, but the people who died in the crash are somehow incidental. They are collateral damage to her dramatic story about red wine and the irreplaceable white top she wore to the concert."

Cue merriment.

I stared into my mirror, eyes narrowing, as if expecting a reaction from my audience—me —but none was forthcoming. Too dark? Comedy can be dark, and people laugh. Is it too ironic? Too derogatory? Too obvious? Maybe I didn't understand humour. Maybe I didn't understand people. Perhaps I overanalyze everything to death, killing the joke and finding myself right back where I started - people laughing *at* me.

Chapter 2 - Jesse

During the summer between high school and university, my father encouraged me to get a part-time job.

"It will build character, son," my father had explained. "God knows you could use some human interaction."

My mother didn't push but supported her husband's stance.

It's not that I didn't want a job. I didn't feel capable of handling everything that would be expected of me. The thought of speaking to people when spoken to was unfathomable.

"Hello, welcome to The Fish House. Have you decided what you'd like to start? Oh, I would recommend the Halibut. It's pan-seared with blah blah blah..." What a nightmare!

Or *"Can I help you with anything? Yes, everything is 40% off today..."* Ick. I'd rather have turned myself inside out.

So, service wasn't something I could manage. Perhaps a back-of-house fry cook, a cleaner, or a farmhand?

In the end, I settled on becoming a farmhand. I was a strong young man with lots of energy to spare. Surely, a farmer would value those traits. Living in a rural area surrounded by various types of farms, I decided to visit each one and leave my name and number in their mailboxes for someone to contact me. Passive, I know, but that's just me.

My mother took the calls, and I completed short interviews using a pre-written letter of responses my father had put together for every conceivable question.

It worked; I had fooled them all and started with a family farm that grew strawberries, among other produce. They also operated a Family Fun Park, which generated revenue by hosting kids and parents during the long summer days. It included trampolines, hay mazes, carnival games, a few kiddie rides, a petting zoo, and, in October, a Haunted Barn.

One day, I was assigned to the trampoline station to ensure that only the recommended number of children were allowed to bounce at a time. Each child had five minutes to enjoy the trampoline. But what if more than the suggested number of children jumped on the trampoline?

It was a balmy summer day at 2:00 p.m. when I made the executive decision to allow more than six kids on the 20-foot-by-20-foot trampoline. The parents seemed happy to have their kids on the bouncer and off their hands for five minutes. Chaos broke out when the number exceeded twenty screaming kids.

No one was bouncing in time with each other. Kids' knees were giving out, and their limp bodies were being thrown into the air, landing on other kids. Pants were falling off, and sandals went flying. Soon, the sounds of glee gave way to terrible screams of fear and pain.

Still, those kids who managed to keep their knees from buckling continued to jump, landing on hair, ankles, and limbs until they realized the extent of the carnage. Eventually, the jumping ceased, and the kids helped each other off the trampoline, assisted by the horrified parents.

The butterflies were racing, and I felt dizzy, so I stepped down from my station to help where I could. It surprised me that even children could recognize the danger in a situation and stop themselves when their peers were scared and being trampled.

A father approached me with fire in his eyes. He pointed at the clearly marked signage, which stated that no more than six children may be on the trampoline at a time.

"What are you even *here* for if you can't obey your own signs?" He shouted over the emerging triage happening around us. Children lay about the dirt nursing twisted ankles, broken glasses, injured arms, and faces, while others searched for lost shoes and hats scattered along the perimeter of the trampoline.

I just stood silently, taking in the bedlam, the irate father's hot breath on my neck. The experiment had outperformed my wildest expectations. When the scene changed from joyous to terrifying, the children acknowledged the perils and stopped for the sake of their peers. It showed a sense of social responsibility. The ages ranged from 3 to 8 years old. No one older than eight or taller than four feet was permitted on the trampoline. So, these toddlers experienced empathy for their fellow kids by recognizing the dangers and shutting them down.

Impressive, I thought, turning and walking away from the gathering of parents backing the angry father. Someone had to be blamed, I'd supposed. I never went back. Not even for my paycheck.

I don't recall sharing such a profound concern for my peers at that age, or any age. I suppose from a third-person perspective, ignoring gossip could be considered a kindness to the target in that I wouldn't be furthering the gaslighting. But that was never my intention.

My intentions seemed to begin and end with causing mischief. After losing my job on the farm, to my parents' chagrin, my mom set me up with another shrink. I'd seen a few in my time. But this would be the last.

"You know, if you don't want to talk, or feel you can't, it's okay," Dr. Ross said after five minutes of silence. Her office was bright, smelled of cedarwood – don't ask me how I know this - and she sat in her corner chair facing me on a comfortable couch. "You can use my notebook to answer my questions."

I accepted the book and a pen from her, barely lifting my gaze to acknowledge the gesture. I hadn't spoken to anyone outside my mom in the past month. It was worsening. I only knew that if I ever wanted to have a conversation again with another person, I would need help. If I ever wanted to feel that connection others take for granted, I would need help. So, I forced myself to speak.

"I'm afraid," I told her, voice raspy, and lifted my head to watch her reaction.

"Good, Jesse," she spoke in a calm, encouraging way. "Could you expand on that?"

"W-what I'm afraid of?"

"Yes."

It took me a moment to gather my thoughts and then another moment to organize my response. "I guess ... everything. I-I mean, well, not everything." Wow, that wasn't worth the two minutes it took to say. The problem was that my thoughts were disconnected from my words.

"I think you simplified your answer," Dr. Ross is smiling, but not condescendingly. She was a professional. She was also very patient. I appreciated that. "You can write your thoughts down if you feel that would better represent what's in your head."

I looked at the notepad in my hand and felt the hard spine bend in my hands. The pen wedged between the pages. It was embarrassing. I was no good at this.

"People," I managed. I don't remember permitting myself to say anything, but there it was.

"Okay," she leaned forward, her comfortable blanket slipping from her waist. "That's a common fear, Jesse. Many struggle with social interaction. It's a source of anxiety. Is it a source of anxiety for you?"

I nod, pleased to be making progress. My grip on the notebook loosened as she connected with my fear. I thought she noticed that.

"What's your method for getting through social situations? Birthday parties, dinners, and back-to-school shopping excursions." She probed. Did I have a coping mechanism?

"Dissociation," I told her.

"You detach from the event. You go inside yourself and just become the observer," she told me, like she'd seen this before.

I nod, "Yes," maybe she *can* help me.

"That's absolutely normal, Jesse," she validates. "Dissociation is a common issue among youth today. It is something you can overcome with calming exercises. Breathing techniques. Tapping. There are many options. Then, once you've relaxed, you can attempt to integrate."

No, no, no, no, no, no. This *isn't* what I want. I don't want to integrate, I decide. I wish only to observe.

This was a mistake, I thought. Dr. Ross noticed my head shaking.

"Jesse, you don't have to rush into anything," she explained in her pleasing way, leaning in. "I understand you're going away to University in the fall. Would you like to learn coping techniques to assist you?"

I sighed loudly and found it difficult to breathe, the room closing in on me. For some reason, her helpful suggestions were having the opposite effect on me.

"Remember, Jesse, what you aren't changing, you're choosing," she stated. "What I mean is, if you're unwilling to make a change, then you're making a choice not to. Does it feel like a choice when you do not interact with others?"

I've asked myself that question many times. Is it really a choice if I'm afraid? Or am I just reacting to the anxiety? I know I could try harder. But do I want to? I feel light-headed.

"Breathe, Jesse," she urged. "Count to four as you breathe in, hold for seven and exhale for eight and repeat."

I heard her, but I couldn't follow her instructions. What the hell was wrong with me? My face felt hot. Was I holding my breath? Things became blurry, and I felt dizzy. Next, everything went dark.

I woke up to my mother and Dr. Ross seated next to me. Mom had my hand in hers. Mine was hot and wet, while hers was cold and dry.

I didn't go back to Dr. Ross after that, and although I know it upset my mother considerably, I didn't agree to see anyone else either. I decided I was meant to be the way I was. I figured I could handle myself better at school by dissociating rather than using learned techniques to help me interact. No. I was what I was.

Chapter 3 - Jesse

My grades were high enough to earn me a spot at a well-regarded university in Hamilton. My mother was proud to see her sensitive boy off to pursue post-secondary education, while my father said little more than 'try to make some friends out in the world.' I knew he cared in his own way. I wasn't the son my father had hoped for; I was awkward, standoffish, and mute around people. The opposite of my dad. Still, despite being surrounded by thousands of students at college and having to share a room with someone other than my parents, I was excited. The butterflies returned with the promise of more stimulating adventures in new yet undiscovered social settings.

Three years into university, at twenty years old, I still find it compelling to observe others sharing intimate feelings and thoughts without the filter I feel compelled to use in every imagined social situation. It's as if each of my thoughts is a planet orbiting a star. Extracting it from that gravity well requires significant energy. For the most part, I don't believe the effort is worth disturbing the delicate balance I've maintained between thought and conversation. If I could communicate via ESP, life would be much easier. Thoughts forming, then appearing in my voice box and travelling over my tongue, teeth, and lips as they contort to express my feelings through spoken sounds seems outdated and absurd.

I'm aware that my outward appearance can also be somewhat off-putting. I'm hardly Prince Charming with my broad head, short, wavy, red hair, long mouth with full lips, and small, green eyes set under a heavy brow. These obvious physical disadvantages gave children ample opportunities to devise nicknames for me in the schoolyard. 'Eyebrows' was one, given that mine are so faint a colour that they're nearly invisible. I likened it to calling a large person *Tiny*. Once, I tried my mother's eyebrow pencil on them to enhance their shape and colour. Children can be ruthless in the 7th grade. I was pinned down in the school yard and had my eyebrows washed off in a dirty puddle.

At twenty, I'm 6'1" with a thick build–not fat, with broad shoulders, and I carry myself with a slight stoop. I lack a sense of style; it never felt worth the effort. My wardrobe mostly consists of T-shirts and jeans–plain black, white, and blue shirts. No graphic T's, no band or cartoon character or quote that resonates with me, nothing to make me stand out or start a conversation about a shared interest. My features are enough to attract anxious looks.

I am majoring in psychology at the university and am writing my thesis on communication. I know how that must sound. What would a mute know about communication? Especially verbal communication, which is my focus. It's what people reveal about themselves when faced with an uncomfortable silence that fascinates me. I don't have any friends and don't want any. As I've observed, friends usually like to share their viewpoints and use you as a sounding board for ideas, and I know this would be endlessly draining. I conceded this a long time ago. I'm here solely as an observer of the human condition, not one who participates. It's like the kids in grade three gossiped: 'Jesse isn't even human.' Still, my fascination with the world outside my reach—including social gatherings, dating, and forming relationships meant to last a lifetime—drives me to learn as much as I can through careful observation.

At my umpteenth college party, I am known as the non-verbal one in the room. Some of the kids think I'm on the spectrum; that's possible, but I haven't been diagnosed. Others have tried sign language on me. Some look at me with disdain, while others feel a kind of detached sympathy. No one wants me at their parties. I'm an enigma—someone to be ignored and discussed in huddled groups. Of course, I'm okay with this. I have a dissertation to write. I'd hate to speak to anyone, and the other kids gave up on me in the first year. Still, there are always new faces, and I tend to gravitate towards them, listening in on their conversations and studying their social cues.

Uncomfortable silences have consistently elicited the most rewarding reactions from others for me. Social gatherings are enjoyable, where people meet, connect, and argue. My presence usually unsettles others. I use this to expose their anxieties. They start asking me questions to calm their insecurities about me. When I don't respond, they fill in the gaps, and my thesis writes itself.

In my observations, I discovered the ability to extract information from these revellers during the uncomfortable moments I create with my presence. As if in contrast to my indifference to speak, awkward strangers feel the pull of my gravity, releasing their fears and insecurities on me verbally. It's been a treasure trove of data for my dissertation.

It's a technique similar to using *the silent treatment*, which aims to promote deeper reflection from an interviewee. It allows them to fill in gaps with content the interviewer might not have considered. For me, creating an uncomfortable or awkward silence goes a step further than the silent treatment. I have placed myself in social settings where conversation and camaraderie are expected. While the silent treatment tests a person's responses under stress, my approach is more intense, as my participant has not agreed to my experiment. They are caught off guard. My tactics reflect the psychological dynamics and emotional control of the subject. Additionally, I do not avoid eye contact. I stare directly into my subject's eyes to elicit a more meaningful response. About 10% just storm off or slink away after a few seconds, receiving no reaction from me. Another 7% become angry or confused, while 1% may become violent. The remaining 82% either share a story or invent one to explain my peculiar behaviour. It's their sharing of a personal story that I'm after.

Alcohol and drugs found at these parties are a bonus because those who indulge tend to lose their inhibitions. This benefits my experiments. I don't drink or use drugs of any kind, not even prescription ones. My parents hadn't taken that route either. My doctor, who was old school, believed I would outgrow my awkward stage, so **ADHD** medication and others weren't even considered at any age.

Of course, autism was mentioned, and there are psychiatric medications to help those on the spectrum better handle societal demands, including selective serotonin reuptake inhibitors like Paxil, Prozac, and Zoloft, among others. I've heard all of them discussed at various times during medical appointments. Another type was Tricyclics, the oldest class of antidepressants, including Norpramin, Anafranil, and Elavil, all of which I remembered for possible future use. But for now, I feel I'm functioning at a level that will support me in my dissertation. Everything has a purpose—whether it's the gossip, the beatings, or parties. I will write an exceptional paper and be recognized for it. No longer invisible. No longer no one.

So, back to the alcohol and drugs. I had not been exposed to such heavy use of substances before arriving at university. It seems like everyone is struggling with something that requires an unhealthy amount of street drugs and alcohol to fit in. Does no one have the courage to show up as they truly are? Does everyone think there is something wrong with them? Are they all overcompensating for a perceived flaw in themselves?

The answer is an emphatic **YES!** My experiments have performed well in class, at the grocery store, and in the bleachers, where I would stare at stone-sober classmates taking in a game. Still, when inserted into a party with dozens of inebriated peers, the experiments become far more accessible. Easier. Quicker in their completion. Parties are where people who don't know me either steer clear of me or introduce themselves. Those categorized as the latter are all too willing to talk about themselves and are often wallflowers, too. It is intoxicating, evoking butterflies in my stomach while I write my paper.

I was invited to a classmate's house party tonight via a group email. I walk purposefully from cluttered room to room, trying to make eye contact with anyone who will meet my gaze. A group of girls coming out of a bathroom on the second floor paused to look at me. They are clearly high, with smoke billowing out the door. That familiar smell of marijuana pervades all these student parties. The open window does little to lessen the stench.

There are three of them. One taller than the next, lined up and holding each other's hands for stability. They are giggling and bursting with artificial joy, reminding me of young goslings left to navigate a busy intersection while mother goose honks from the opposite side.

"Oh," the brunette is the first to react, placing a hand over her heart. "Well, you're a surprise!"

I take this as my cue to start another experiment. I tower over all three, unmoving.

"I think you stunned him, Brynn," exclaims the false blonde, nearly falling backward if not for her friend's tight grip on her elbow.

"Well, you're a tall drink of water," Brynn says with a faux southern accent I find irritating. "Cat got yer tongue?" She bats her fake eyelashes that complement the accent.

This is how it begins. They want me to say something. Anything. But I won't. Maybe this time I should? The faux blonde is stunning. Maybe she'd entertain sex? I hadn't allowed myself that experience yet. No. Right now, I'm writing my thesis, and that is enough.

Brynn, the brunette, slides a soft palm up my bare, freckled forearm. She makes a noise that denotes pleasure. "You're a solid build, aren't ya?" She smells like a combination of weed and essential oils.

The redhead leans into her friend, eyes too far apart but on me. "What could you do with a man like that, Brynn?" All three eye me up and down. The blonde wannabe bites her lower lip.

I feel myself harden at the prospect of bedding all three, and the girls notice immediately. They giggle at me. I'm sure they are not laughing *with* me, as I'm not laughing. I feel myself flush. Are they laughing at the size of it? Is it too small? Laughably large? I'm getting feedback, but it's difficult to concentrate with a raging boner bending hard right down my pant leg.

The redhead gasps, "It's sooooo big!" They laugh again. So, it's bigger than most. Or is that sarcasm dripping from their glittered lips?

I fight the urge to run, to hide, as that would end the experiment prematurely, and that's not who I am. I'm a professional who shifts my hips to allow the boner to arch upward, freeing it from my underwear's elastic hold. I know I'm making a pained expression while completing the procedure.

"Oh, honey, don't be shy; let's have a look," Brynn says, her eyes falling on my erection. "Can I have a look?" She nods as if allowing herself to touch me. Next, she takes my hand, and I reluctantly follow her into the bathroom, where she closes the door. I've never been in this situation in my twenty years and feel the familiar butterflies, but this time lower than my abdomen. I let Brynn push up against me as her delicate fingers work my button and zipper. My hands are beside me, gripping the edge of the countertop, fingernails digging into the soft wood beneath the laminate. She slides her hands into my pants and pulls both my jeans and underwear to my ankles in one fluid motion, landing hard on her knees with a thump. I'm betting she's done this plenty of times before.

Next, she struggles to remove my pants entirely, pulling off my shoes, and I step out of them, my hands wet with sweat, sliding along the countertop. My boner is the biggest I've ever seen, and it feels as if it will tear the skin at the head.

"So big," Brynn mumbles, fingernails against my thighs. A wisp of her hair brushes against my penis, and I feel a release I've only ever felt from a wet dream as ejaculate bursts forth, landing in Brynn's thick, dark hair. It covers the top of her head and keeps giving. It's a geyser. I'm confident this is not how she had envisioned this ending. She gasps as the ejaculate dribbles onto her forehead, landing atop her fake eyelashes, forcing one eye closed.

Brynn huffs and snaps, "Oh. My. God. You've ruined my hair, you idiot!" She shoves me aside and turns on the tap, dunking her head in the sink. Meanwhile, I dress hurriedly.

"I'm not your fucking *tissue*, you oaf!" Brynn is angry, but I'm dizzy and not really listening. "Jesus, cum faster next time!" She jests. I couldn't help myself. Wait, will there be a next time? "Premature much?" Premature ejaculation, she means. That's not a good feeling. And wasn't I supposed to pleasure her as well? I decide to even things up and start to work on her skirt while her back is to me.

Brynn turns in a rush of hair and water to face me. "NO! W- what? What do you think you're doing?" She's spitting daggers at me.

I can't answer; I want to explain myself, but my jaw is frozen. My hands rise to placate her.

"Get the fuck out of here, you freak! I don't want you touching *me*!" Brynn glares at me until I understand her message. "Get. The. Fuck. Out!" she yells, eyes wide. I'd suggest a shower, but I won't.

I struggle to buckle my belt and trip over my shoes as I rush out of the bathroom. Brynn's girlfriends are nowhere in sight. I walk through the hall and down the stairs, throwing myself out the front door and bumping into several people out for a smoke or vape.

The walk home only increases the confusion. Shouldn't Brynn have wanted me to return the favour?

Isn't that what being romantic with someone means? Had she only planned on pleasing me? Why? Was I charity? That made sense. Whatever the reason, this is new data for my dissertation, which would require me to add an extra chapter and possibly reorganize what I've already completed. This should upset me, but instead, I feel the butterflies return.

Chapter 4 - Jesse

Back in my rented basement in a suburb of the city where I attend university, I lie in bed listening to the sounds of the elderly couple who live above me. Instead of staying in the dorm where I had made too many of my peers uncomfortable over the past three years, I convinced my mother, with as few words as possible, to let me move into a rented room just a short bus trip from my school. Mom is always so supportive, hopeful I'll find my way, and if a basement apartment might help, she is willing to pay a little extra. I honestly doubt my father even knows I'm out of the dorm.

I have minimal interactions with the couple upstairs. This is for the best. I lock myself away in my basement apartment, which includes a bedroom, a washroom, and a kitchenette. The house is on a wide street with homes built in the 1940s. The neighbourhood features a small park with a recently added splashpad, a discount grocery store where I can shop, various fast-food options, and a billiards bar.

I can't sleep, so I decided to go for a walk. During this walk, I pass a small bungalow, seemingly out of place amongst the older, attractive homes, packed with people.

They spill out onto the single driveway, smoking cigarettes and vaping frantically. It seems like an adult party, probably a birthday or anniversary, I think. I wonder how old the guests are and whether I could blend in if I altered my course.

Then, a new, sinister thought occurs to me. I wonder if I can sow enough doubt and anxiety to create rifts in established relationships and make people feel uncomfortable in their own homes. Would their secrets come to light as they shout at me to leave the safety of their home? It wouldn't be the first time. I've been asked to leave parties, nearly assaulted, and shown the door dozens of times because of the nervous energy I carry. It's not about frightening people—only about observing their reactions to silence in social settings. If their reaction is fear, so be it. What ugly secrets does society hide when someone outside the norm is thrown into a celebratory atmosphere?

Moments later, I find myself standing in the middle of the road, staring at the activity inside the house through its large bay window. The streetlights are burnt out, making me invisible to them. This could be my chance to prove or disprove that similar outcomes occur in more mature environments. Would the uncomfortable silences I create lead to me being thrown out of this party? Would they call the police? Or would they accept me, and would their tolerance level be more evolved than that of a university student? These unanswered questions fuel my curiosity.

I move toward the merrymakers without a second thought and enter the 60s bungalow. I walk through a small crowd in the expansive kitchen, find the living room, and sit in an empty chair against a wall to watch and wait. The butterflies slam against my sternum in anticipation.

Three minutes later, a man in his thirties, I gather, probably the host, notices me sitting in the corner and asks my name, embarrassed that he doesn't recognize me. I remain silent, barely acknowledging him. The host laughs it off and turns to find support, perhaps from his wife. I watch him scan the living room, but she's not there. He then refocuses on me, whom he cannot place.

"You're a neighbour kid from down the street," he tells me, wagging a finger. "I think I remember seeing you mowing your lawn." I stare at the host, expression revealing nothing. I've never mowed my landlord's lawn. The way my small eyes fall in shadow under my heavy brow from the pot lights above makes the host look away. I have used this technique before. It produces great results.

"Where's Lilly, uh, that's my wife; you must know Lilly," he turns his head, careful not to turn his back on me. "Yeah, she's probably in the kitchen. Did you want a drink?" Nothing. "I'll get you a drink." He rushes to the kitchen, and I think a water would be nice, but how long can I keep up this charade? The experience is thrilling. I'm tingling inside. This is much better than the student parties, where other hosts often tap out before revealing anything.

"This is Lilly," the host says, returning with his pretty, 30-something wife, who has large, staring eyes, wearing a cotton top pulled down her shoulders and an attractive necklace that complements her neckline. "Lilly, you must know our neighbour," he's telling her rather than asking, having convinced himself that I'm their neighbour.

I can tell that Lilly doesn't want to embarrass herself by not recognizing the man seated comfortably in her home. "Uh, yes, hello, I never got your name." The host looks satisfied that his wife has confirmed the mystery guest and waits for me to reply with my name. Anything, my acknowledgment would be enough. But I reveal nothing. I look from one to the other, recalling another of my nicknames from elementary school – 'Beady Eyes.'

"Oh, here's that drink," the host pushes a glass of clear liquid toward me, ice cubes clinking together, but I don't flinch. "No? It's a gin and tonic. It's the house drink." He laughs uneasily. Lilly looks at her husband and nods, her face creases with a pensive smile.

"I'll be in the kitchen. Jeff, why don't you check on the *others* and see if they'd like a refill?" The host, Jeff, nods, happy to be given a task that doesn't involve convincing me to talk. He smiles nervously and turns to engage the others.

I can see Lilly in the kitchen and watch her from the corner of my eye as she touches and strokes the backs of other men while they talk to her. She's laughing, but it feels forced. She's all but forgotten about me. I watch a man's hand brush past Lilly's outer thigh and notice the look of lust in her eyes as she licks her lips, pausing with her tongue slightly out, then brushing her hair off her neck as she makes eye contact with him. It's all a game. I feel for Jeff.

I wonder if I could make a friend here instead of continuing with my experiment. I might say, *'Thank you, Jeff,' and accept the drink. 'No, I've never met your wife, but you seem like a lovely couple. The warmth from your lights through the bay window and the sounds of merriment set my course, not a familiarity with either of you.'*

Of course, I can't just open my mouth and say such pleasantries, can I? The challenge of overcoming that phobia makes that scenario unlikely. So, I keep on with my research.

Soon, I noticed my host questioning other guests about the mysterious man in the green, mid-century modern chair. Many eyes take turns squinting or briefly engaging with mine from across the room. The anxious feelings I had managed to induce in Jeff excite me endlessly, raising goosebumps over my freckled forearms. The host returns moments later.

"It's odd how I can't quite place you," he begins, leaning against the updated wallpaper while stirring his gin and tonic. You know we've lived here for almost a year. A year in August, actually, Lilly and I." Nonsense talk. I maintain my practiced poker face, which unsettles those who feel compelled to speak with me.

"I thought I'd have seen more of you. I mean, I'm not here all the time either, but on weekends," he pauses, "I don't work weekends, and we spend as much time outside exploring the neighbourhood as we can. I'm Jeff, by the way. You obviously know Lilly." I don't offer my hand to shake because it's too late for that formality. I've been at the party for half an hour, and the host should know the man sitting in his chair.

"I'm in the insurance game. I'm an adjuster," he says. Is he running out of small talk? "It's why we moved here. It's a nice city. Artsy. We're getting our bearings. I imagine you've lived here longer than we have." He knows by now that he's not going to get an answer to his question and moves on.

"How is it, you know, Lilly?" Jeff realizes his mistake in asking another question and answers it himself. "Just from the street, I guess. I'm not prying. You've maybe had a coffee together?" I sense Jeff's fear bubbling to the surface. Has Lilly given Jeff cause to question her fidelity?

"Lilly enjoys meeting new people. I'm not the extrovert she is." Jeff clears his throat and shifts his weight onto the other leg. "We haven't always been happy, Lilly and me. She's had her flings. You probably don't want to hear that, but it's true. We came here for more than just my work," he takes a shaky sip from his glass, "we came to escape a past." I blink once, my face emotionless while the butterflies flutter wildly in my chest. A tingling sensation sparks, and I almost smile. Jeff is teetering on the edge of revealing a bombshell.

"Wow, I don't know why I told you that," Jeff bounces himself off the wall with a push of his muscular back to stand upright. "Are you a religious man? You're quiet, that's for damn sure." Jeff goes on to answer his questions. "Never known a Monk before," he laughs uneasily again, looking into his glass. "Maybe you're not a

Monk, eh?" His eyes grow dark. "Maybe you've known Lilly longer—" he swallows thickly. "She seemed hesitant when she saw you here." I could end his growing suspicions about Lilly, but that's not what this is about. This is about understanding the human mind—and watching it fill in the blanks. Fortunately, they most often fill in the missing pieces with their fears, the basis of my paper.

"Fuck," Jeff whispers, his head nodding almost imperceptibly, "that's why you're here. You're telling me she's at it again." Jeff isn't drunk. He's just paranoid. A cheating spouse will do that to a person. If I've learned anything from my psychology courses, it's that the victim never gets past it. It's always the first thing that comes to mind if they can't get in touch with their partner or haven't returned when they said they would. It's sad, but even more so that the wounded party wants to make it work after the betrayal.

"If you know something, you'd tell me, right? We're neighbours. Men," Jeff's hands alternate, moving between us, spilling his G&T, appealing to our shared gender and supposed proximity. "It's not you, though, right? It's not you she's *fucking* on the side?" Jeff's lip turns up as memories of her infidelity surface on his face. "You wouldn't come into my house and flaunt it in my face like this. Christ, what are you, 18?" Jeff is becoming flustered, pacing in short circles beside me. I wonder where this will go, butterflies thumping against my sternum. Adrenaline is pushing through my veins. Blood pounding in my ears. Jeff's voice rises above the instrumental jazz and muted chatter.

Lilly turns the corner, her anxious gaze landing first on the husband she's once betrayed and then me, who Jeff now thinks has been fucking his wife. Jeff notices the way Lilly looks at them both.

Jeff turns to his wife. "So, we move a thousand klicks, and you're still not happy," he yells, his fear surfacing, arms rising at his sides. "I tried, Lil, I really did, but if you're intent on ruining our lives, then fuck you!" Jeff lowers his accusing finger and rushes past her. Her mouth is agape, amplifying her stunned look. She gives me a final, questioning, scowling stare and turns to follow her husband out the front door. I knew couples kept track of their partners' misdeeds, squirrelling them away for moments like this—moments when they could use them against each other. It's the illusion of a perfect relationship crumbling here. It's the truth laid bare. Lilly will likely use whatever transgressions she's squirrelled away of Jeff's against him to defend herself. It will be messy, but necessary. Whatever therapy they had after Lilly's indiscretions did not achieve its goal. Jeff is still suffering, and Lilly must suffer in turn.

I feel energized by the results of this experiment. I'm buzzing from head to toe. I won't stick around to see if Jeff becomes physically violent, but Jeff doesn't strike me as the violent type. He's a victim, and needed reminding of that. Maybe he'll finally leave her and find someone better suited, more loyal.

Whatever Jeff's endgame is, it's none of my business.

Chapter 5 - Jesse

After sneaking out of Jeff and Lilly's unhappy home, I walk the short distance to my rented basement and start tapping rapidly on my keyboard, recording the data from my brief encounter at a 30-something's party.

With this new content, I have added depth to my thesis. I can now comment on three distinct age groups: teens, twenties, and thirties. I paused and thought about how much more I could include in my paper by placing myself in different generational settings. I could visit nursing homes for the 80s and 90s demographic and lawn bowling clubs to capture the atmosphere of the 60s and 70s. I might also enter a corporate environment to represent the 40s and 50s. The possibilities seemed endless.

I stand and wring my hands with excitement over this breakthrough. The work I've been doing for the past three years has been necessary, but it has centred on a single demographic. Why confine myself to teens and early 20s when there's a whole world of experiences to explore?

I minimized my thesis, opened my search engine, and searched the internet for senior housing facilities in my area, finding three. I run a hand through my loose carrot top and scratch furiously. I haven't felt this alive since my time with Brynn in the bathroom. Of course, I won't mention her name in my dissertation, nor Jeff's or Lilly's. I must protect my sources and myself from any legal fallout. Not that anyone would have a case. I hadn't spoken a word, just let their reactions unfold. There are no Good Samaritan laws to worry about. Even in those moments where I was shoved, ridiculed, and beaten, I wouldn't give up names. It was all for the sake of science. It wasn't about the individual but about the reaction.

On Sunday, I visited one of the homes for the elderly and sat in the common area at the front, where staff wouldn't ask me questions. They would assume I was waiting for my grandma. It isn't the staff's reaction I am analyzing today. The common room features a grand piano and multiple seating areas where residents can sit and socialize with one another. A young girl is tapping a familiar song from a bygone era on the piano keys. Her supposed grandmother watches proudly, chatting with her peers.

I sit in a high-topped chair in a group of four, facing each other to foster camaraderie. Two women lean over their armrests to better hear each other gossip about their long-deceased husbands. After a moment, they notice me and turn, revealing their bright smiles, their yellow teeth smeared with lipstick. I stare in their direction. The women, in their 80s, seem content to wait for me to introduce myself.

I assume my trademark demeanour, staring without a hint of emotion. I give nothing away. I feel somewhat cruel for the silent intrusion, but I won't relent.

"Oh, hello, dear," the woman to my right says, leaning in with a visible shake in her right hand. "We didn't mean to be rude. I didn't see you there at first." They both look on eagerly for a response to her greeting. They expect the common courtesy of a reply. And why wouldn't they? It's a societal norm. But I'm not looking for conversation.

"Are you here to visit someone, Pet?" the other woman, with her snow-white hair thinner than my father's and a strong Scottish accent, asks.

I say nothing in response. I'm not feeling butterflies in my chest. Instead, I feel oddly anxious. Maybe this was a bad idea. I don't want to scare these poor women.

"Odd you're not speaking, Son," the woman to my right says, her tone and expression concerned. She turns to the other woman, and they exchange a sad look.

"Is it that you can't speak, Pet? Are you dumb?" the other woman asks, using an outdated term that now carries a much more derogatory meaning. Her face shrinks into the middle as her eyes narrow to focus.

"Oh, Helen, you can't say things like that," the woman on my right scolds. "Helen doesn't mean anything by it, dear. She's from another time. You know she's eight years my senior."

"Oh, stop telling everyone that," Helen says sharply. "You're always going on about your age as if you're not a dried-up old husk like the rest of us here in this godforsaken place."

"I'm defending your use of the word *dumb*, Helen, so he realizes how out of touch you are."

"This is what every conversation turns into when a man sits with us," Helen tells me. "Marilynn has to make me look the fool to win the man's affections!"

"When you use old-fashioned terms to explain a condition, I *defend* you by explaining -"

"You aren't *defending* me, Marilynn. You're scolding me again, so you look like anything but the old bag of that dust you are! I've told you not to do that. I know my mind and said what I said because it fits!"

"Helen, the word means something more than you remember. Like *Fag* isn't a cigarette anymore. It's a term for homosexuals." Marilynn rolls her eyes.

"Well, they've absconded with the entire alphabet, so why not rob us of *Fag* as well?" Helen scoffs.

"Oh, for heaven's sake," Marilynn leans back into her chair. "I'm so sorry you have to witness Helen's bigotry like this, young man. It slips out more often than not these days." Her finger taps at her temple.

"Oh, don't apologize for my sake, Marilynn! I can speak for myself. He's a clever lad and can see through your nonsense."

"Nonsense? You'll be transferred to the assisted care wing if you're not careful. Most believe you're already dealing with dementia."

I feel that was a hurtful comment to her friend, and Marilynn adds, "She won't recall I said that by dinner, dear. Don't look so worried."

Do I look concerned? I raise a hand to my frown. That won't do.

"Ach, you're *dobber*, Mary," Helen says to end the argument, crossing her arms so they sink between her sagging breasts and rounded abdomen.

Marilynn pulls a tattered tissue from the sleeve of her knitted sweater and dabs at her petite red nose. "I miss my friend sometimes, you know," she whispers. Helen glances her way suspiciously.

"No secrets, now," Helen insists under her breath.

"She can't hear worth a damn either, not really," Marilynn says, dismissing her comment while still leaning into me. "But I do miss the old Helen. The Dementia came on suddenly, and it's a cruel disease. It takes your memories and often brings out the worst in some. Helen was likely raised with bigotry and racism in the old world. Now, she doesn't understand any differently."

I'm fascinated by how these women have simply accepted my presence, the awkward silence, and everything that comes with it. Is Marilynn also struggling with Alzheimer's or Dementia? Is this how older people typically behave? Are they so desperate for a conversation with a new face that they're willing to do all the talking?

"You look like a thoughtful man," Marilynn nods, leaning back again. "It's those who don't ramble on who can offer something more substantial when it's their turn." She winks over her bloodshot eye. "I've known one just like you. He'd say, *You don't learn anything by talking.*"

Is Marilynn trying to place me in a box she finds familiar? This is an exciting development. Goosebumps rise on my forearms.

"My Thomas didn't say a word until he was seven. They call that non-verbal nowadays. But he's fifty-nine now and has had a marvellous career as an engineer," she pauses, but I don't believe she expects any reaction from me. "Thomas was never one for people, however. I think that might be the trade-off where genius and society part ways. Never wanted a relationship. Never spoke of a family or children. The work was enough."

I watch Marilynn's eyes glaze over. She's been deprived of her perceived right to be a grandmother by Thomas. Pragmatically, I think, her tears will help alleviate the redness associated with what I perceive to be dry eye.

"Mind you, he's a lovely boy, but he's never had a friend in the world. Never wanted one, I suppose." She looks directly at me. "You neither, I suspect." Her eyes narrow, but a knowing smile graces her thin lips. "If I had to guess, you'd be a carbon copy of my Thomas."

Marilynn dabs her tissue at the corner of both eyes, leans in again and places a cold palm on my knee. "Don't live in fear of others, dear. You miss out on so much."

A tea trolley arrives, and Helen receives a hot tea served in an ornate China cup on a saucer, accompanied by two biscuits. Marilynn also notices the cart and helps herself to tea, slipping three biscuits into her pocket. She then turns to me once more and tilts her head.

"Life is short. Take it from an old woman, dear. Every day passes more quickly than the last. If you don't surround yourself with people and experiences, I'm not sure what it's all for." She takes a sip from her cup and remarks to Helen how well-steeped the tea is. Helen agrees, her mouth full of dry cookies crumbling from her loose lips.

I've never known my grandparents well, since one set lives in the UK and the other died before I was 8. However, today's experiences with these two elderly women have provided a wealth of information for my thesis. I also feel I've gained some wisdom from someone who has lived. Perhaps my grandparents would have shared similar advice, but advice is only helpful if it is followed.

This experiment is over, I decide, and I stand. The young man with the tea trolley, roughly my age, asks if I plan to stay for tea. I glance down at Marilynn, who looks up at me. We exchange a knowing look, sure that I won't stay. Marilynn nods barely perceptibly, acknowledging my decision, and turns to the teetotaling man. "He can't stay, dear. Much to do today." She winks at me, and I can almost hear sandpaper rubbing against wood as the dry lid fights to moisten the arid eye. I feel the butterflies tumbling around.

I leave the building and spend the rest of the day online, looking for activities suitable for people in their 60s and 70s.

Chapter 6 - Jesse

Less than two months remain in the school year. A snowstorm accompanies the end of February. Winter is going out like a lion. Schools are closed, but my class curriculum is uploaded to our online login. I use this time to research potential meeting spots for people in their 60s and 70s.

A curling club five blocks from my apartment is hosting a meet-and-greet tonight to attract new members. This presents an opportunity to test with different age groups in another experimental setting. It will add data to my expanding paper and deepen the work.

The storm had passed by seven o'clock in the evening, and the sidewalks were cleared. I headed to the club for the meet-and-greet in its upstairs bar area. The air outside was cold, and my breath fogged in fits, but the wind had quieted, and the streetlights cast a strange glow on the evening. It made me feel like the night was hinting at something ominous.

Upon arriving, I stomp my boots to shake off the sticky snow and scan the room with a deadpan expression. I notice a man I estimate to be in his 70s, wearing a sweater adorned with my university's logo, gazing at the curling ice beyond large floor-to-ceiling windows that run the length of the bar. The ice below is illuminated, enticing new members. People move about along the length of the ice. I'll admit the scene is inviting. Something about the calm, cool interior under heat lamps draws me in until I find myself standing in the far corner near the 70-something man. His eyes dance in the reflected light of the windows, though his heavy eyebrows must hinder his view. Maybe he's reliving a Bonspiel where he took the cup or whatever signifies a curler's highest achievement.

He notices my reflection in the window and nods with a grunt. I give no reply.

"You looking to join?" he says at the window in a stern, detached tone. "It's good to have young blood in an old sport."

I stay silent. He takes a sip from his plastic cup, disturbing its contents. The scent of alcohol is released. I remain perfectly still with my hands folded in front of me, staring at the ice.

"It's calling to you, the ice, isn't it?" I catch him glancing at me through my peripheral. "Has you under its spell." He says matter-of-factly, drinking deeply from his cup.

"She's a siren that way. Calls to you. Then she breaks your heart." He clears his throat. "Full of stories, a sheet like that. Epic wins. Crushing defeats. Can you hear the Lead's cry? Like a ghost summoning you to play once more upon the strip."

This one has a flair for the dramatic, reciting cantankerously, but I keep any emotional reaction to his narrative in check. I feel he speaks more to himself than to me, but is glad for the company.

"Take her in," he drains his cup. "She has other secrets to tell. If you look closely enough, you'll find more excitement beneath the sheet than above." He leaves me with this riddle, and I struggle to understand its meaning.

Was something buried beneath the ice, or *sheet*, as he called it? Was there a greater mystery to its construction? Was it built over an indigenous burial site? Maybe the ghosts he mentioned were real rather than metaphorical. But then, are ghosts ever real?

Regardless, that was an impressive speech from a gruff 70-something reminiscing about his glory days on the ice, and sound data for my paper. He shared a wealth of content simply by allowing me to be in his space. Now that he's gone, I feel drawn to the ice. Others are walking along the side of the sheet. I join them.

The air is cooler in the rink. I move along the rubber carpeting lining the left side and listen as others talk.

"One hundred fifty by sixteen and a half feet to one lane," a man, I'd say in his 30s, testifies to an attractive, dark-skinned woman of a similar age. "That's the Hog line there," he points confidently at a painted line beneath the ice while leaning on a broom.

"Interesting," the young woman replies, clearly unimpressed. I figure she's his date. I don't see it going further than tonight. But what do I know?

Should I try experimenting on them? The idea is undermined by the lingering question of what lies beneath the ice. What might the old man have meant? Perhaps a body? Someone who offended the wrong Bonspeiler - if that's a word.

As I walk across the rubber padding, studying the painted lines and circles beneath the thin layer of ice, I sidestep people holding drinks. Why does the old man's comment suddenly matter so much to me? It's beyond my purpose. I am here to explore the human condition, not to crack a puzzle.

Then I see it: a gold coin with a waterfowl relief on its shiny surface. The coin is in the center of the circle. It is repeated along all six of the rinks. I recognize it, of course. It's a one-dollar coin. A Loonie. Is that the secret? What's the mystery? Who put them there? Why? Maybe a good-luck token? Then, a poster of the Canadian men's gold-winning Olympic team from 2006 catches my eye. Alongside it on the same wall are photographs of a man dressed in his Canadian gear, placing the coins before the rinks were flooded here.

I don't think the old man who gave me the riddle was very fond of this permanent installation. Maybe it was the athlete who placed the coins he disapproved of. I suspect he opposed it, at the very least. Not the exciting mystery I'd hoped for. But a mystery solved, I suppose, nonetheless.

Chapter 7 - Jesse

As February drags on and my paper keeps writing itself, I can't get the old man at the curling club out of my mind. How could someone speak so cryptically over a few Loonies trapped under the ice? I feel he was alluding to something more. He was clearly drunk. Maybe smashed, as my peers say. If I've learned anything from my experiments, it's that drunk or high revellers tend to reveal much more than they would if sober, like they'd been fed a truth serum. I just don't know how to follow up on the old man's words. Being non-verbal, whether by choice or design—the jury is still out on that—will make it difficult to ask questions.

My dissertation is nearly complete, and shortly, I will have more free time. The gamification of my uncomfortable silence experiments is starting to feel monotonous. Currently, I find myself merely going through the motions for the adrenaline, which doesn't seem very professional.

One of my professors referred me to a colleague who can help me improve my speaking skills. He called him a miracle worker, which is what I would need to speak to anyone other than my mother or myself.

Maybe it's time to step up and get involved in the game of life instead of just watching from the sidelines.

On a Friday, I walk down the stairs between stadium seating in Professor Klein's lecture hall. He is seated at his large desk. The room is empty. The lights are mostly dimmed, save for the one over his desk. I was asked to see him after class. It has taken considerable courage for me to approach anyone on this subject. The severe lighting places the professor in shadow as he mulls over the papers before him.

I'm unsure how to bring up my issue if I don't speak out, but I have a feeling he's been briefed. He looks up and sees me standing with my hands by my sides.

"You're Jesse," he says to me. I nod. "It's a brave thing you're doing." I appreciate how he's already offering affirmations. "You've shown courage despite your disability. Finishing three years of college must have been quite challenging. But you're almost there." He stands. A neatly trimmed, greying beard and thinning hair frame his kind, round face.

I shuffle my feet. *Don't waste this opportunity by experimenting with Professor Klein,* I order myself. *You want to be more. SPEAK!*

"You don't have to talk right now, Jesse. We'll get there. Right now, let me speak." With a wave of his hand, he invites me to sit in the front row and takes a seat two seats to my left. "Professor Saunders has filled me in on your details. He says you're a bright lad with a bright future."

That's a glowing review from arguably the most decorated professor here, I think. Saunders has been published in several notable journals and even appeared on a TV special.

"However, that bright future will depend on whether you can effectively connect with your patients, assuming you want to pursue a career in this field." I nod. I do want that. The human mind fascinates me, and I have learned many techniques to help people navigate their various challenges.

"Good. Then, we must first determine why you have chosen to forgo verbal communication. You communicate through the written word. Professor Saunders has provided me with your work from the last three years, which is very insightful. You have no trouble understanding new ideas or generating your own. You might be on the spectrum, but I'll conduct some assessments with you to better understand where we're starting from. You'll be asked to write about your childhood. Could you tell me about your upbringing and the circumstances in which you grew up? Are you comfortable with that?"

I nod, feeling foolish that I can't speak to this intelligent man. It's humiliating. I've never felt humiliated due to my inability to speak. This is a new reaction. Perhaps an honest one. I wipe away a tear. Emotional responses are not my thing. Why am I feeling so much?

"Listen, Jesse, your intelligence isn't in question here. Being non-verbal isn't a measure of intelligence. It's a reaction to one or more events. It's often a choice, and we can make different choices. You do it all the time." He returns to his desk, picking up a full binder and handing it to me.

Telling me that being nonverbal is often a choice resonates with me. It was a choice. Is it still a choice, or have I lived with the same choice for so long that it has become a habit? Right now, I could choose to speak, but I am afraid that if I try, I will fail. I would like to speak with this man. I want to show him I'm not this mute. But all at once, I don't.

"Answer the questions and return the binder to me when you're finished. How you respond to these questions and scenarios will give me insight into your condition. Some are standard autism diagnostic queries, some relate to selective mutism, and others aim to explore how your personality has developed over the years and how it influences your decisions."

I stand and nod, my eyes sweeping across Klein's face, acknowledging his efforts. I'd be lying if I said I wasn't a little excited about the prospect of being normal. I hug the binder to my chest and try a smile. It probably goes unnoticed.

"So, when you're finished, I'll be here. Don't overthink the questions. Just answer honestly, and we'll have a solid foundation." He rounds his desk and takes a seat. "I look forward to working with you, Jesse."

I nod once more and depart, my footsteps resonating in the spacious room.

In my basement apartment, I reflect on my meeting with Professor Klein. My uncomfortable silence did not deter him, and I was nervous. Changing who you've been for so long is not an incidental matter. However, the professor was prepared and quickly took control of the conversation. He is an experienced professional—a professor and practising developmental and personality psychologist. I feel lighter after meeting with him. I opened the binder he'd given me and began working on the questions.

Chapter 8 - Jesse

Even as I work through Professor Klein's binder, my thoughts drift to the old man and his mystery at the Curling Club. It feels silly to revisit the one-sided conversation, but something nags at me. The resolution about the Loonies seems too straightforward. The way the man's jaw was set and the intensity he brought to every word felt too genuine to be about something so simple.

So, then, what? Is there a bigger mystery behind this? Should I investigate it more? I pull my laptop over to my desk and close the binder. I Google the name of the Curling Club and click on the News tab.

The search page first shows last weekend's membership drive. Then, there was a serious COVID announcement. Next, a small fire at the club in 2019 was followed by another membership drive in 2013, a roof renovation in 2010, and finally, a visit from the Canadian Gold Medal team in 2006. Nothing indicates a mystery. I continued scrolling and then found an article about a missing person's case, naming the Curling Club.

The photo is in colour but grainy, taken in February 2006. This stirs the butterflies. Perhaps there's more to the old man's mystery after all.

A club member, Carly Reese, was reported missing by her husband after an evening celebrating a regional win at their location off King Street, between Grant Avenue and Tisdale Street. The husband and everyone who attended the celebration were questioned extensively. Additionally, the police questioned the losing team.

Another article from March 2006 features a plea from Carly's husband, Joe Reese, appealing to the public for help in finding his wife. It includes images of a police line moving through a frozen field with flashlights, dogs scenting through the woods along the lakeshore, and Joe standing at a podium outside city hall with the Police Chief beside him.

I lean closer to the screen for a better look at the husband. It could be the old guy who spoke to me at the curling club—just twenty years younger. It's hard to be sure. I tried to remember his eyes, but they were difficult to see under the thick eyebrows curling inward, rolling over his wrinkled eyelids.

I look again at Joe Reese's eyebrows in the grainy photo on my screen. They are thick, but whether they curl isn't clear. I find it hard to believe Joe ever manscaped, but he was younger then, and maybe his eyebrows have grown out since. What else? His hair? It was a wiry mess that night—salt and pepper, like dried corn silk. I remember wanting to touch it briefly.

Shifting focus back to the photo, I notice Joe has a mullet. That's not helpful. His thick dark hair doesn't resemble the old man's either.

I zoom in on Joe's shirt on the screen. It displays the insignia of my university. The butterflies flutter against my ribcage. The old man was wearing a similar sweater at the club—an alum sweater. The logo flashes in my mind, and I watch it attach itself to the logo in the photo. Bingo.

He must be one of those people who enjoy others knowing where they studied and with whom their loyalties lie in the college sports scene, but that's the only commonality among the men. Likely, it's nothing, but I'm feeling the adrenaline now and need to shake it out of my arms. It's as if I've overdosed on my experiment. As if I'd simultaneously encouraged an entire party to share their darkest secrets with me. It's overwhelming. It's extraordinary. It's got to mean something.

I decided to investigate Joe Resse further. I need to discover his link to my school and see if he is the same grumpy old man from the curling club. I immediately sat back down at my desk and visited my university's website to look for Joe Reese in the alum section. Maybe his picture has been updated.

Two people sharing the last name Reese appear. I click on Joe's profile. My heart is in my throat. I'm covering my mouth with one hand as if to stifle a scream. Like I'd make a sound. No picture. That's disappointing. However, there is a brief biography of the man. He graduated in 1978 with a degree in Psychology. The same course I'm in. A chill assaults my spine.

That feels a bit too familiar, I decide. Bordering on creepy. I suppose this is how some people feel when I run my experiments. Creeped out. I'm not sorry that I experiment with live subjects. Still, I understand that it can evoke unwanted emotions, like the one I'm experiencing now, where my brain and body tell me something isn't quite right and that I should tread carefully.

There are no updates to follow on the alum page for the faceless Joe Reese, so I minimized that window and opened another. I checked Facebook, but I couldn't find anyone in the area with that name who has an account. I suspect he's too old to use IG or TikTok, but I check to be sure. Resting my chin on my hands, a strained groan escapes from deep within my throat. Staring at the screen, my eyes grow heavy, and I drift off to sleep.

Waking up to the sound of my morning alarm, I lift my hands behind my head and stretch. A deep crackling in my spine sends blood to my neck and face. I almost black out, shake my head, and stand. I gulp down the room-temperature half glass of water on my desk and rub my eyes.

I shower next and drag myself to school. I pass Jeff's house, as I do every weekday. I feel remorse settle in my gut. I wonder how they might be managing his outburst at the party that night. At least there have been no police cruisers stationed in the driveway. I pull my parka hood over my head to hide my shame. Had I gone too far with that? My body is telling me I had. But the butterflies that night were telling me to push harder. Urging me to get him to spill everything. The thought that perhaps the butterflies were bats caught me off guard. That's dark. But I hadn't expected him to go off like he had on his cheating wife. That added another dimension to the experiment.

They say you can't control what's happening at any moment, but you can control your reaction. Jeff had so much pent-up anxiety over his past that even the slightest hint that his wife might be going outside the marriage again made him snap.

Heck, maybe he needed that. Needed me. But now I'm just comforting myself. I almost wish I could speak. I would explain myself. I would confess. Maybe a letter. But does that open me up to legal action? Is what I do illegal in any way? Surely not.

At school, I see Professor Saunders before class. If I had to choose my mentor, it would be this man. He has my best interests at heart. I have finished the binder of questions that Professor Klein, his friend and colleague, gave me. Saunders nods, and I sit at the front of the classroom. He walks towards me.

"Professor Klein told me you've started the assignment he prepared for you." Saunders stands over me; a satisfied expression animates his features while the pot light above ignites his white hair in a halo.

"I'm glad you're taking this as seriously as you are, Jesse. The benefits will be priceless." He offers a kind smile, nods his head, raps his knuckles on my desk, and moves to the whiteboard as other students file in.

At lunch, I sit at a computer workstation in the school's library to further investigate the Reese woman's disappearance. The thought that she might be beneath the curling rink's ice has my curiosity running wild.

The idea that the old man revealed his darkest secret to a stranger while lost in his memories helps me craft a very satisfying storyline, certainly not for Mrs. Reese, but as a side project to keep me busy while I wait for Professor Klein's assessment.

I open a new search tab on my personal Google profile, and as often happens, past searches flood my screen. Selective mutism has been a constant in my searches, as I look for new treatments and techniques that could help me communicate in uncomfortable situations. It's always the same, though. What is most upsetting to me is how it will affect my work life. I've managed my educational life quite well. Still, I don't have a social life, so when school ends and I need to enter the workforce, I worry about my ability to function effectively.

I decided to search for the missing woman on social media, thinking she might have had a Facebook account in 2006. Carly Reese shows up in the search results only four times. All the information is from 2006 about her disappearance. Disappointing.

Next, I check YouTube. I search for Carly again and find a few hits. It's footage of the search for Carly Reese from a Vlogger who took her video camera along on the organized hunt for the missing woman.

The Vlogger talks throughout the entire twelve-minute video. She narrates Carly's backstories as she walks through heavy snow along the icy lakeshore. I move on to the next vlog, which features the Curling Club and the Vlogger discussing its history. The 2006 Canadian Olympic team's visit is briefly mentioned.

Then, *bingo*, she's interviewing personalities from the Curling Club. Could Joe be one of them? I moved the timeline forward to see if I could recognize Joe or if she'd added names to the list. It turns out that this vlogger was thorough. A younger Joe Reese stares at me from my paused screen. I recognize him from the news article and now see the resemblance to the old man at the Club.

I push back from my desk, the squeaky wheels of my chair snapping me out of my reverie.

Chapter 9 - Rob

A freshly single dad at 40, I'm hoping to keep the only home my daughter has known. To do that, I needed to rent a room. It's not a big house, but it does have a finished attic and a beautiful inground pool, which we absolutely love. The property is lined with cedars and gardens with enough grass to kick a ball around and play with our dog. So, one can appreciate that we don't want to move as spring begins its long march into summer.

Nearly a century old, our house has stood on Hamilton's east side on Grosvenor Avenue, South, since the 1940s. The double red brick was supplied by the local brick maker two blocks away on the escarpment behind the railway tracks, where a fair number of container cars pass through daily. Behind the tracks are hiking and biking trails, which I enjoy. Mountain biking has been my passion for years. I can cut across the tracks and find myself in the woods in under two minutes following the Bruce Trail. It spans several hundred kilometres, and I could ride east all the way to Niagara Falls or, heading north, to Tobermory through Ontario's expansive Greenbelt. My house has undergone numerous renovations, including my own, which have included a new kitchen and roof over the past year.

Aileen, or Ai as she prefers to be called, came to me in my time of need, responding to my online ad after my wife and I split. My ex lives just three blocks east of me in a house we owned as a rental property. My ex and I have tried to make the split as amicable as possible, given that we have a beautiful toddler between us, we feel it is best to remain friendly.

My wife left me for a much younger man. I know, flip the script, right? I question everything now, of course. I'm hurt; the split is relatively recent. I have my moments of doubt, where I ask myself what I ever saw in her. However, I recall that initially, I was drawn to her artistic inclinations. I always felt, and still do, that art—whatever its medium-is an essential part of being human. She made it clear after the unravelling of her theatrical dreams that the whole endeavour between us was a mistake. Still, we stuck it out, had a daughter, and separated shortly after. I hadn't seriously considered splitting up once we had our daughter, but I now realize that was never far from her mind. Call me dense, call me an unfortunate optimist, call me what you will, but I believe in family values. In hindsight, we never shared those values, and so the split was—and still is—the only thing that makes sense.

After moving to Canada with her new Canadian husband, Aileen - that's the name my tenant chose to appear less foreign or more Canadian, or simply to avoid confusion with the abbreviation for Artificial Intelligence. However, I'm not entirely sure which. Her Japanese name is Ai. It means 'love' or 'affection,' yes, I looked it up. It appears like this in her native language: あ. So, it wasn't a big leap for her to call herself Aileen, which means

'Shining Light'. When I told her that, she blushed. Her smile is enchanting. Ai is a tall, slender woman of 33, with a pale complexion, short jet-black hair, and a kind, round face who tends to make herself very small. She doesn't take up much space, and I sense a shared kinship in her pain.

She had fled her white-bred husband, whom I came to learn was an abusive prick, and had snapped at her one too many times. This husband of two years was a mama's boy whose mother disapproved of Ai in his life. Her racist mother-in-law made it impossible for Ai to fit into the family dynamic and even went so far as to instruct Aileen's new stepdaughter to be cruel to her.

Ai came to Canada in good faith to learn English and build a life here with her new husband and stepdaughter. Not long after she arrived, her stepmother moved in with them, and so Ai's struggles in Canada began.

After she left her husband to her mother-in-law's satisfaction, Ai worked as a Personal Support Worker, or PSW, while learning English. In late spring, she arrived at my door to rent the attic room, which included a shared bathroom and kitchen.

She has been with me for two months now, and yes, practicing her English has involved sharing her life story. Aileen and I have had a few conversations over tea about our recent pasts.

My daughter, Katie, now four, enjoys having a female presence in the house again. The house, however, holds other feelings. Perhaps it isn't fair to say, 'the house,' as the ghost hadn't died in my home; at least, that's what he passed on to Ai. Ai, who declares herself a notorious ghost magnet.

Chapter 10 - Aileen

English is a complex language to master. As a recent immigrant through a marriage to a man whose personality changed the moment I set foot in Canada, I quickly realized that learning English would be the least of my struggles.

My mother-in-law hated me the second I stepped off the plane, and I watched my new husband's expression fall as they picked me up from the airport. He looked horrified at first when he saw the look on his mother's face upon spotting me. Did she expect me to be a white woman like her? This was an odd expectation, as she knew I was arriving from Japan. Had Sean not explained to her that I was Japanese? This was a bizarre realization. Had he not shared a single photo from our wedding?

She said nothing to me as we drove to Sean's house, my house, in a fancy downtown Toronto neighbourhood. I was excited, yet tired, and eager to meet my stepdaughter, who was with a babysitter while Sean picked me up from Pearson International. When I met her, she looked just like the photos Sean had shared with me over the last year, and she was so sweet, handing me a favourite stuffed toy and telling me I could sleep with it.

My mother-in-law snarled at the kind gesture. Sean's smile quickly faded again when he noticed his mother's reaction. My heart sank even as I knelt to receive the gift. At least I wouldn't have to see my new mother-in-law very often, since she lived north of Toronto. Then the announcement that she, too, would be moving into the house to help with expenses felt like a nail being hammered into the coffin of my burgeoning marriage. I had no illusions about winning this woman's affections with my pleasant manner. She was clearly against this marriage. Sean must have felt empowered while living and teaching in Japan for the last year, his mother unable to control him from afar when he decided to marry me. Was it merely an act of opposition toward his mother? Was I?

I forced a smile at the news and awkwardly hugged the wretched woman, welcoming her into what I believed was my home. She quickly made it clear that it wasn't, and that I had no right to feel comfortable inside its walls. I told Sean about this, but he insisted we needed her here to help pay the bills. He expected me to take care of the house and his daughter, so I wouldn't have a job outside those duties. Suddenly, I went from thinking I'd barely see my mother-in-law to feeling trapped with her 24/7. That's when she began souring the idea of me with her granddaughter and son.

After a month, I tried to explain to Sean that she was an unreasonable woman, and I couldn't live with her anymore. I didn't give him an ultimatum, but it was implied.

"You don't work," he shot back. "We need the money to stay in this house!"

"I'd be happy to move to something more affordable," I begged him. "I can't live with her constant judgment. She's cruel to me," I told him in my broken English, which made him seem more defensive of his mother - as if I were the outsider here.

"Why can't you two get along? She loved Laura," his first wife. Of course, she did. Laura was everything my mother-in-law would have looked for in a daughter-in-law, and they'd both fought cancer, but Laura lost that fight, and Sean left for a year to figure himself out. I met him through the school where we worked. Sean was teaching English while I prepared lunches for the children. At first, I thought it was selfish of him to leave his small daughter after such a traumatic loss. But she was with her grandmother, he assured me, and that was better than if he were moping around feeling sorry for himself. Besides, he'd said, he had always wanted to experience Japan.

We continued to see each other through school events, and then, more personally, when he asked me to dinner. Looking back on our time in Kyoto, I realize those were some of the best months of my life. I fell in love for the first time. It was magical. We got married after five months of him courting me, and he returned home for good, with me following soon after. And now, here we are.

Maybe I could have confronted his mother and stopped the toxic behaviour, but the fact that Sean's deceased wife kept visiting me, shouting for me to leave her family alone, was more than I could handle. It took me one miserable year, but when I told Sean about my experiences, he dismissed them as stress-related and said the coldest thing he'd ever relayed to me: that maybe I should leave.

This was the dirt thrown onto the coffin of our marriage as it lay in its cold, black pit. I felt sick over his refusal to believe me and his disinterest in working on us. It took me a month to leave him, as I secured a job and a room in a neighbouring city on the opposite side of Lake Ontario. Hamilton. A blue-collar town of steelworkers with a vibrant health care and arts community. My landlord, Rob, was recently separated and had a beautiful daughter living with him 50% of the time. The price was right, but I did have to share the family bathroom and kitchen. Rob seemed kind and happy to receive me. Grateful even. The opposite of my husband.

I quickly realized that, despite that encouraging difference, not everything was as it appeared. The ghost haunting Rob's home was eager to share everything with me.

Chapter 11 - Rob

After a couple of months of Ai living in the attic, we'd become friendly, and when our schedules allowed, we'd have dinner with my daughter. Over these months, I could see that the lines in Ai's face had relaxed. This made me glad. My pain had subsided, too, and I had been on a few dates. I was going on one tonight and pacing in the backyard under a hard sun. This woman was met through a dating app that hadn't yet borne fruit. So, my skepticism, even after a few weeks of online chatting, was at an all-time high.

"Why do you worry so much, Rob?" Ai said as she brought her laundry out to dry on the line. "You have nothing to worry about."

"No?" I asked, chewing on a nail I had just clipped. "I guess I'm not worried, but maybe just nervous."

"Is this not the same meaning?" Her expression tightened as she tried to understand the difference.

I laughed and shrugged. "Sorry. I guess it is." I inhaled deeply and exhaled. "I'm going to a pretty expensive place tonight. It's in Burlington. I drove past it last week and then made the reservation. There are lots of good reviews online. I guess I should pay for dinner."

"Why must you pay for it?" Ai had a funny way of asking questions. Very innocent.

"First date and all that. Wouldn't you expect the man to pay?"

She deflects by suggesting, "Maybe you should have met for coffee or lunch first?"

"Maybe," I pause to appreciate the logic in this. "Too late now, though."

"You will have a nice time," Ai begins, nodding her head, her bottom lip protruding as she attaches another tiny shirt to the line, "and you can tell me all about it later." Her optimism is appreciated. We tend to support one another. It's a good living relationship.

The date went well. The restaurant's atmosphere and the food were excellent. The conversation primarily focused on our failed marriages. Misery does love company. I paid for dinner, which included two bottles of wine. Apparently, commiserating over shared rejection went best with a couple of Italian reds. Then, in my car, we kissed.

I was disappointed to realize there was no genuine passion. There was enough lust to get us through the night, but the connection we'd built was that of two displaced people missing a physical relationship. It's disheartening to say. However, I did take her back to her place. And I did stay until the early hours of the morning.

Ai is improving, though I still notice moments where she misses the connection she once had with her husband in Japan. Should we date? That might be ideal, right? Or would it just be a relationship of convenience? We live in the same house, sharing the bathroom, kitchen, and even the living room—which I now refer to as the common room. We share a lot, especially our recent histories. We also talk about trivial things. That's helping Ai, and I tell her that her English improves every day. Where once she comically mistook the dog's name for mine over dinner, she now rarely makes a grammatical mistake.

Ai is a good soul. Her expectations of coming to Canada to build a life with her new family were innocent. I think we're all innocent when we start on a new path. Excited to begin again. Offering the benefit of the doubt. Maybe that feeling should be described as naivety rather than innocence. I believe that getting involved with Ai on a level beyond our landlord-tenant relationship would be naïve. I see this with each new date I go on. You enter with innocent expectations, but reality sets in when there is no reply the next day or the week after. Besides, Aileen and I still have more healing to do.

Chapter 12 - Aileen

That night of Rob's date, I heard him enter the house just after 2 am. He's quiet and considerate. I hear the dog, Jackson, scrambling on the kitchen tile to meet him, the back door opening to let him out, and the television turning on - the volume quickly fading away. I'm studying for my next test in my nursing course. It's a very challenging program. I managed to take a nap from 7 until 9 tonight, knowing I would be awake for most of the night, drilling the Latin names of the upper torso into my brain. Another language to learn!

Rob retired at 2:30, and somehow that comforted me. I feel secure under his roof. I feel safe when he's home. But even when he's not, I have Jackson, the golden lab mix, to give me comfort. Rob is a thoughtful man, tall, standing at least 6'2", as I am 5'9". He has a distinct style that typically features blue jeans and a t-shirt that may or may not include a graphic of some obscure band or movie. His features are masculine, framed by a square jaw, arching eyebrows, and a full head of brown hair. He is very handsome by anyone's measure and carries himself on a lean, yet muscled frame. I have wondered if we should date, but I fear that might be too convenient. Creepy even, to hit on my landlord. Because, as comfortable as I am with him, he is still my landlord.

As night turned into morning and the moon sat high in the sky through my skylight, I found myself nodding off. Then, the ghost appeared. Rattling on beside me, he lay on my bed with one hand supporting his head, as if it weighed anything!

Chapter 13 - Rob

The following week, Ai approaches me with a tired frown, sitting heavily at the kitchen island with a huff. I turn from my scrambled eggs on the cooktop and ask what is wrong.

"I don't know if I should bring it up," Ai says, her head hanging.

"Is it the bugs? "We had an infestation at the start of the week, but I called in an exterminator right away. Stink bugs. Beetles from China. An infestation!

"No, not the beetles," she says, her eyes meeting mine. Dark circles are starting to form under her eyes. "It's ... I'm worried you won't believe me."

"Try me."

She takes a deep breath and exhales shakily. "It's the ghost. You have a ghost, and he won't leave me alone. He lies beside me and talks so fast I can't study for school." She takes another breath and looks at me, troubled.

"I-I don't know how to react to that," I say plainly, my head shaking unconsciously. Then I realize that is not a fair reaction and say, "I'm a *believer*, I should have led with that, but a ghost in my house is – I hadn't expected it!" I force a laugh, and goosebumps follow.

Ai appears shaken by my reaction. I take a breath and lower my tone. "So, what does he say to you?" I put down the spatula.

"My English is not good enough to understand when he talks so quickly." Ai seems defensive.

"Have you experienced this before?" I am trying very hard not to sound condescending.

"Yes, they are attracted to me, to my energy." Ai shifts in her seat uncomfortably. "They know somehow that I can see them. Hear them. So, they want to tell me things."

"What sorts of things?"

"Who they were, what they did in life," she looks bashful. "Who they loved. But -" she pauses.

I feel like there's a lot more to come. "But?"

She straightens up and leans in, her forearms resting on the countertop. "Last night, I made out that he had instructed me to have you remove the carpeting in your daughter's room. I got the sense that he was concerned about asthma."

"No kidding," I say, dumbfounded. No question, the carpet throughout the house was old, but could it really bring on asthma?

Ai's carefully manicured brows furrow as she leans back, studying my expression. "You don't believe me."

"No, I do; I believe in ghosts. Honestly, my aunt is heavily invested in that world. We have the best conversations."

Ai's expression shifts. She realizes I'm telling her the truth. "I'm so glad you believe me. It's so hard to tell anyone about my experiences." Her hand is on her chest. "It means a lot to me, Rob."

I nod, "And if he's bothering you when you're trying to study at 3 in the morning, send him down to me."

"Do you mean it?"

"Sure," I don't expect to experience Ai's ghost as she does, so why not? I don't share that particular gift, much to my aunt's discontent, and if it will help her get through the next few months with her nursing course, I'm happy to oblige.

"I'll tell him next time he makes it hard for me. Thanks, Rob."

I shovel the eggs onto my plate and sit at the island to eat. Ai makes herself a tea and tells me she's heading out to work. I contemplate what she's told me, consider whether I can afford to remove my daughter's carpet and install a vinyl floor, and consider seeking a second opinion on the ghost from my aunt.

Chapter 14 - Sandi

Walking through Gage Park Greenhouse, I remember my childhood pet, Thumbelina. As I watch the painted turtles swim in the artificial pond alongside the goldfish, a sudden flash of memory hits me. I was 8 years old and had two pet turtles. They lived in my bedroom, in an aquarium with several large rocks for basking in the warmth of the heat lamp. I was playing in the yard with some friends when, suddenly, I felt a gut punch while sitting on the lawn, pulling dandelions. I stood up so quickly that my head spun for a moment. "My turtle is dead," I announced and ran inside.

"Where are you going, Sandi?" my friend Sabrina shouted.

"My turtle is dead!" I yelled back, tears streaming down my flushed cheeks. Sure enough, when I reached the aquarium, Thumbelina, my female turtle, was dead. I tugged at her tail and legs, but nothing moved. Usually, she would have retracted her limbs quickly. I picked her up, and her head hung limply to the side. I cried and cried until my mom had to send my friends home and help me dig a hole in the yard for Thumbelina.

But that's the life of an Empath. Empathy opens doors to the unknown, revealing what is hidden and evoking all the emotions. It can be exhausting. As a psychic medium, I utilize empathy to reveal the unseen world and illuminate it for others. I help those grieving understand that this life is not all there is. This life is the physical reflection of the universe. It is where souls experience the physical realm—to learn, suffer, and find joy through a distinctive perspective.

Developing empathy is challenging when you don't engage with others' experiences or have your own. If you live only for yourself, you'll find it hard to connect with others. That's why people in the health care sector, like my nephew, dedicate themselves to helping others. They understand various types of pain, including physical, mental, emotional, and otherwise. They recognize suffering and strive to help.

Artists, as another example, are full of empathy. They radiate empathy, which shows in their chosen medium, whether that's music, visual arts, dance, or other creative forms. It's transformative, and that's why certain musicians connect deeply with people, why their music resonates with them. It's why some artists' paintings act like roadmaps, revealing truths about someone who never expected to have an emotional response to the work.

This is why humanity needs art, because we need empathy. Without it, only self-interest remains, and that benefits only the narcissist.

I point out the fish to my great niece, Katie, whose father was kind enough to leave her with me for the day.

Rob has been separated from his ex for – what's it been? A year now? 2? Katie's parents seem to have a copasetic relationship and mutual love for my niece. I've tried to forgive Rob's ex-wife for leaving him. Maybe I have. Their daughter is an absolute joy to be around, regardless of the trials their split may have caused her. May continue to cause her. But growing up in a household where the parents are constantly at each other's throats is a worse way to grow up, I think.

Rob mentioned he wanted to discuss something with me over dinner when he picks up his daughter. For the life of me, I haven't been able to read him on this request. Rob, too, is somewhat of an empath. It's in the family. His mother, my older sister, is a very empathetic person, but never sought to expand on the gift. Some fear it. Some just don't want to know the secrets that hang over all of us like a dark veil ready to drop. I don't pretend to know why my sister has chosen to ignore the nagging universe. We don't discuss that. The closest we came was when our father passed. We both experienced vivid dreams of him. Though they were different, they affected us similarly, and she, too, realized the significance behind the message Daddy left us. Mother too. Our dreams differed again, but they offered similar meanings upon her passing. Regardless of her indifference to fully embracing our shared gift, Loren, like Robbie, is happy to listen to my experiences. I am inspired by the hidden knowledge that is offered to me through my gift. I consider it an honour to be able to peek into the Akashic record and represent those spirits willing to communicate with their loved ones through me.

This gift has been in my family for generations. Even my mother, sewing in the family room decades ago, once saw my grandfather at the front door after hearing a knock and being answered by my grandma. When mother looked up from her sewing, she saw her father, my grandpa, who had died years before. She told me he smiled, waved, and disappeared before her eyes. My grandmother did not share in that vision, but my mother swore up and down that it was her father, whom she had not had the opportunity to say goodbye to before he passed.

Shortly after that encounter, at 12, while playing croquet with a friend in the front yard, I saw my paternal grandfather drive by in his small car. The man and the car disappeared as it moved down the street. I remember feeling faint and having to sit down. I ended up falling hard on my friend's foot, spraining her ankle.

So, my gift, though frightening to a child, was accepted from the start. I believed in my abilities early on because my eyes bore the proof that others might overlook. I don't accept unbelievers into my practice and can sense one a mile away. It's not because I wouldn't love to change their minds, but because I don't have the time to give them. Never have. If they think me a swamp witch, so be it. I'm not here for them to question my intentions.

Ghosts have been a part of my life, and from an early age, I chose to accept that instead of running from it. I'm 79 today. My husband is peacefully passing away at a hospice not far from my home in the city where my nephew lives. My children are in Winnipeg, where they grew up. My husband and I moved to Ontario to seek treatment for his rare cancer, but it advanced so quickly that we stayed in our rented house in Hamilton to continue treatment. Now, he is in hospice, and I'm grateful to have Robbie and my sister nearby.

As we walk along the path inside the greenhouse, my niece points to a beautiful flower called the Bird of Paradise. I kneel next to her, taking the bloom in my hand, my knees popping like cherry bombs as I complete the descent.

"Auntie, you broke your knees!" She exclaims, wide-eyed.

"Oh no, dear, I just have very loud knees." I smile, winking at her, and she smiles back. This little girl will share in my gift; I can tell just by her aura. She is a little wonder. Rob told me she once described a rainbow surrounding his head. I explained to him that she was likely referring to his aura, the electromagnetic energy around a person that reflects their spiritual, personal, and physical well-being. I can see these auras too when I focus on someone. A rainbow aura, in particular, is very rare and signifies a healer. It makes perfect sense since Rob wants to heal the world. Considering his recent circumstances, he is also a Registered Massage Therapist with a very positive outlook. He doesn't give up. Rob has given many massages to his uncle to help him through the relentless treatments he's endured. We are grateful beyond words for his generous spirit. I see our coming to Hamilton as kismet, with the treatment and Rob here to assist as my husband transitions.

Chapter 15 - Rob

At my aunt's, I pull up to the sidewalk and park in front of her tiny bungalow. Built in the 1950s, the interior was renovated about five years ago. Flipping houses has been big business in Hamilton over the past twenty years. Although small, the rent was affordable, and that's all Auntie was looking for, hoping the treatment would go well and they could return home to Winnipeg. I'm glad that the house is nice, though, since they've been told that my uncle cannot be moved.

I feel sad for my aunt and my cousins in The Peg. Sad for my uncle, but relieved he's in such a good place. It is well reviewed, and the people are truly lovely. I've volunteered some time to give massages to residents when the staff thinks they might benefit from a relaxation massage. It seems like the least I can do.

My daughter is wearing a tiny chef's hat that my aunt bought for her birthday last year. She loves to cook, my girl. She has baking powder on her round cheeks and a smile that lifts my spirits. She hugs me and shares her day with me. I hug my aunt. We're a family of huggers, and she's one of the best. It's never a quick tap on the back but an all-encompassing squeeze. I squeeze her back, and we sit in the charming family room, where a whitewashed fireplace serves as a centrepiece.

"I've a question for you, Auntie," I say from the little couch, leaning forward, my forearms resting on my thighs. My daughter is playing on the floor in the corner, and I lower my voice so she doesn't hear. "It turns out that my new tenant shares an affinity with you."

My aunt leans forward from her recliner. "For butter tarts?" She teases. I laugh. This woman always makes me laugh.

"That's a no to the butter tarts," I reply, calling up Ai's slim build. "But rather your ability to see ghosts."

This piques my aunt's interest, and she sits straight-backed in her chair. "Oh? Isn't that curious? This is the girl from Japan?"

I nod. "Aileen, yes. She has told me that I have a ghost. In the house." I lean back and pull one of the embroidered pillows onto my lap, tracing the embroidery with my finger.

My aunt's eyes narrow as she considers this news. "I'm surprised I didn't sense a presence when I was last at your house. Perhaps this is a recent addition."

"All I know is that Aileen has been distracted by this guy trying to tell her things. Her English isn't perfect, and she's at her wits' end. I don't want to lose my tenant over this."

"So, you're wondering if I might come and take a look?"

"Please. Yes. She was very specific about something he'd told her." I prepare myself to explain my daughter's room and the rug when she pulls it out of thin air.

"Asthma," she says without hesitation. "He's worried about asthma."

"That's right." I feel a chill crawl up my spine. "How'd you -"

She waves me off. "It's what I do, Robbie. It's who I am. Of course, I will come and talk with your ghost."

"Great, because he wants me to pull up the carpet and replace it with hardwood or whatever. So, it would be good to know whether Aileen heard him right."

Dinner was a store-bought BBQ chicken that my aunt had me carve, along with mashed potatoes and peas. All in all, a nice meal. I then picked up my daughter and headed home to the city's east side.

When I arrive, Ai is pacing the short distance between the front and back doors in the hall. She is upset. I send my daughter to her room to get ready for bed and ask what is bothering Ai.

"It's the ghost," she offers, her hair a mess, eyes wild. "He followed me today, Rob."

"Followed you? Do you mean he left the house? Is that a thing? I thought ghosts haunted one place."

"It's very rare, but it happened today. He got into the passenger seat of my car and talked to me all the way to my work. Then he stayed in the car until I came home. Now he's in my room. I don't know what he wants. His voice is so rough. It's like driving over loose stones."

"Gravely," I offer.

"Yes, thank you. Like a gravel road."

"Does he not listen to you at all?"

"No, he only talks," she's exacerbated. "He talks and talks and talks, and I don't understand many of his words." She stops pacing as I gently take her arm and guide her onto a stool in the kitchen. "I can't do my studying. He's taking all my free time."

I fear she's about to start pulling out her hair as both hands run through her jet-black tangles.

"I have my aunt coming tomorrow night. Like you, she's a medium." I watch her expression shift. Relief washes over her face as she reaches out for my hands, gripping them firmly.

"Really, Rob? That is amazing. I would love that. I don't even know his name."

"Okay, you can sleep on the couch down here if you'd like. Bring your computer and study. Maybe he won't bother you for a few hours. Otherwise, send him to me if he'll listen."

"Oh, I will, Rob, thank you." She brings my hands to her forehead and bows. "Thank you, thank you."

"Okay," I can't help but chuckle at her unnecessary gratitude. Occasionally, her flair for the dramatic catches me off guard. "I'm going to get Katie to bed and then get some sleep myself. Early morning. Remember what I said. Send him to me."

Ai nods again and heads to the third floor to collect her belongings. I hope she finds some relief. I really can't afford to lose her. Besides, I've become quite fond of her.

A cool breeze on my bare back wakes me at three in the morning. I shiver and try to pull the covers higher. I realize my back is not exposed, but I'm getting colder by the second. I try to return to sleep, but am pushed. *PUSHED!* No joke. I mumble something and hear my daughter fussing in the next room. The push comes a second time.

"Okay," I answer the push, still half asleep and roll over in bed to see who is shoving me. No one. Nothing. I'm alone in my room, and my daughter is waking up from a nightmare. I shiver from the cold pocket in my bed and the thought that some invisible force has pushed me. "Okay, okay," I tell it. Him? Ai's ghost? *My* ghost.

I lie down in my daughter's room and tell her a story in her tiny bed—the story I've used since she was a baby— where the bed magically turns into a car that can also fly and visit places like Cloud City and other such delightful nonsense. She loves it, though, as her vivid imagination takes over. My descriptions become more appealing, and my voice softens as I point out a puppy pile in a particular cloud for her to land on and snuggle into until she falls back to sleep.

When that mission is completed, I return to my bed, which no longer feels cold. I cover myself with my comforter, feeling a mix of sleepiness and outright fear over the real possibility that I've just had my first encounter with a ghost.

Chapter 16 - Aileen

Pleading with the man to leave me alone and visit Rob tonight works. He listens. Or at least that's the impression I get after an hour of peace. With my studies finished, I manage to sleep soundly until my phone's alarm wakes me.

After I shower and get dressed for the day, I find Rob in the kitchen, his daughter sitting on a stool with a hot chocolate, and Rob toasting bread. The smell is warm and inviting.

"Hey, good morning, Ai, I bet you had a decent sleep last night." Rob seems animated.

"I did, thank you," I reply, feeling suddenly guilty. "Did you not?"

"I asked for it," he laughs to himself. "Your friend visited me." He's buttering the toast now. "Katie was crying from her room, and he alerted me."

"Oh, wow, yes, he seems very taken with her." We both look at his daughter, spooning the hot chocolate into her mouth. "How did he wake you? Could you hear him?"

"No, he crawled into bed with me, froze me out, and then, when that wasn't working, pushed me."

"Pushed you!" This is a profound statement, as ghosts who alter physical reality are classified as Poltergeists.

"Yup, what's that called? A Poltergeist?"

"It is,"

"Like the TV show? Isn't that ... bad?"

"It's powerful, but not always bad. I don't get the impression he is evil. He just wants to, uh, get his story across?"

"Freaked me out if I'm being honest." Rob sets a plate of buttered toast and a jar of honey in front of his daughter.

"I'm so sorry, I didn't believe he would actually listen to me." I feel bad for having woken him in the night. I, too, hear his daughter occasionally wake up unhappy at night, but she always manages to fall asleep again within a few minutes.

"It's okay, Ai, I don't mind. It was a kindness he showed to Katie, so I'm not mad at him. It's kind of neat. She's got a guardian angel right here in the house."

I smile and pull out a pot to make my oatmeal. I'm glad Rob's so easygoing. He's partly why I tolerate the ghost. If he weren't so friendly and understanding, the cheap rent wouldn't be enough to keep me here.

"You're aunt, she's coming tonight?"

"Yes, she will be here after dinner to sit with us in your room and do whatever she does to pull information from him."

"Wonderful. I look forward to meeting her and perhaps helping him cross over."

Chapter 17 - Sandi

A punch in the stomach—that's the feeling I get when I realize something is wrong. When I look at a person, that gut punch might be accompanied by a sensation that they will not live a full life. For some reason, whether it's an accident, illness, or something more violent, their life will end prematurely. This, I don't see as a gift. It leaves me feeling helpless. I could explain my feelings, but I couldn't give them a reason or a timeline. So, what's the point?

I often feel frustrated by this practice. A nurse at the hospice, where my husband is spending his final days, triggered this feeling a month earlier. When she stopped coming, I asked about her. I wasn't surprised when they told me she had suffered a brain aneurysm and passed away the week before.

I only hope she left her loved ones with happy memories to reflect on and that her final words weren't borne out of anger. I wish that for everyone. Still, I understand that having no regrets when you're gone is often just a matter of luck. That's why I tell my loved ones how I feel as often as I can.

The hospice itself is a challenging environment for me to be in. So much death. So much imminent death. I feel sick to my stomach half the time I'm here. I try to ignore it as much as possible, close myself off from it, but the overwhelming feeling in the place is death. Death and kindness. Those who work and volunteer here are dedicated individuals striving to make a positive difference in the lives of those at the end of their journey. It's admirable work, and I know how fortunate my husband and I are to have him here. So, I do my best to focus on the good and not the confusion, anger, regret, and sadness that inevitably walk these halls.

I leave my husband's bedside to join Robbie, his daughter, and the tenant. I'm eager to communicate with his ghostly guest, even though they're rarely truly guests, since they've invited themselves to stay. Still, they often seem confused and might not even realize they've passed. It can be an emotional scene, having to explain that.

I've brought along a few trinkets that might help coax the spirit out of hiding if necessary. Not a Ouija board, though – that's where I first began my journey into the occult.

Over the Christmas holidays in my teens, my cousins and I used a Ouija board in our grandparents' basement to summon a powerful spirit. We asked our great-grandmother, whom we'd known and who had lived to be 102 years old, to communicate with us, but the spirit we received was very different. It answered questions about things none of us could have known until they happened. And when they did, our reactions were layered with fear and dread, and we all agreed never to play with the Ouija again.

Even so, I was not frightened off that easily. After the final unknowable thing was revealed, I broke the promise I'd made with my cousins and bought myself a Ouija board from an antique dealer.

Soon, I had Tarot cards, a Ouija board, pendulums, and other trinkets, enough to start my own business as a psychic at a circus or fair. I was tuning myself into the frequency of the unknown. I was honing skills I felt naturally drawn to. The payoff has been nothing short of extraordinary.

Not all my premonitions come through intuition; one arrived through a vivid dream. When my husband and I were newly married and out with another couple, we were introduced to a woman who joined us at our table for a drink. No unusual feeling overwhelmed me until later in the week when I dreamed she was killed in a terrible car crash. Not another week had passed before we ran into the same couple while shopping, and they told us that the woman we'd met through them had died in a car crash the day before. I was surprised, but even more so that I'd dreamt of the tragedy rather than felt the gut punch upon meeting her.

This type of premonition never occurred again, but I began paying closer attention to my dreams afterwards.

As I drive to my nephew's house on the east side of downtown, the escarpment thick with trees along the right side of the road, I am reminded of the first time I saw a ghost with my daughter. It was an evening spent walking from one cottage to another in Dunnottar, a village on the shore of Lake Winnipeg. I was strolling along the dark trail with a friend and my daughter when I noticed an ethereal figure—a transparent, shimmering glow like that of a full moon—floating near a large cottage that faced the lake.

In a composed tone, I said, 'Do you see her?' and my daughter and friend looked in the direction of my pointing finger. My friend didn't see her, the ghost, but my daughter did. The woman was dressed in a long, white cloak with a full hood.

My friend then shone his flashlight in the direction of the woman in white, and she vanished. My daughter and I exchanged a look as my friend questioned what I'd seen. That night in our cabin, my daughter and I had the same talk my mother once had with me, and her mother had with her. The women in our family have a long history of seeing the dead. We're clairvoyant. We possess paranormal abilities that go beyond simply sensing spirits, allowing some of us to receive messages and interact with the deceased.

Like my sister, my daughter has done everything to avoid this ability, while I have embraced it. I don't fault them for it. Ignoring spirits makes life easier than welcoming them. Why add to the confusion of a life that is already so complex?

I wonder briefly how difficult it will be to connect with Robbie's ghost. He'd made it sound as though the ghost spoke in tongues, confusing his tenant.

But Robbie also explained that his ghost is persistent no matter how much his tenant ignores it. So, I suspect I won't have much trouble joining the conversation.

Chapter 18 - Rob

"Hi, Auntie." I greet her with a hug, kissing her soft cheek. I call her Auntie for brevity. Aunt Sandi seems too formal, and we're anything but formal. So, her title becomes a comfortable and familiar "Auntie." As I pull back, I notice a flicker of excitement behind her blue eyes. It's playful, eager. I've seen it at Christmas as she watched others open presents. She's eager to unwrap my little ghost story tonight; her energy discloses that much.

"Robbie," she takes my hands in hers and breathes in deeply. She steadily releases her breath, smiling all the while. "I could feel his presence the moment I got out of my car."

"That's perfect," I tell her as Ai rounds the corner. "Oh, this is Aileen," I shuffle to the right so they can meet. My Aunt takes Ai's hands next, and I watch them share a moment. It's rare to meet another who communes with ghosts, and I imagine they are communicating a myriad of emotions to each other.

"So nice to meet you, Aileen," my aunt says with a squeeze of her hands. She is the most genuine person I know, next to my mother. "We're going to get to the bottom of this tonight."

My aunt's reassurances to Ai are evident in her expression. Ai appears elated and relieved, as illustrated by the anxiety melting away from her brow.

"I'm so thankful you agreed to come and that Rob believed my story."

"Well, he's bought into my stories enough over the years. So, it's no wonder that he believes in ghosts!" Auntie laughs, and Ai smiles, looking in my direction. I feel a little embarrassed, but that's on me.

"Would you like a tea or something stronger before you start?" I have this compulsion to offer beverages to anyone entering my home.

"No, dear, I want to experience your visitor without any outside stimuli," she says, glancing around the foyer into the family room and the kitchen. I sense she's sniffing out the spirit. She releases Ai's hands and wanders the main floor.

"He's been in my room since I returned from school," Ai offers. Auntie's hand slowly rises to stop her.

"Let me get a sense of his intentions." My aunt peers out the back window in the dining room, eyes narrowing. "I'll go upstairs now." She knows her way around my house, having visited many times since relocating with my uncle. We follow my aunt up into my room, the bathroom, and finally my daughter's room, where Katie pulls at the carpet. I still need to address the carpet situation. I pick her up and set her on her bed.

"Auntie, auntie," she screams, jumping on her bed. My aunt hugs her and tells her to settle down now, as she is here to inspect the house. "I'll play with you in a little while, sweetheart. Why don't you set up your Barbie house, and let's have a wedding? Dress your dolls, and I'll see you shortly."

This sets my daughter to work. As we start to go up to the third floor, where the ghost spends most of his time, my aunt stops me at the bottom of the stairs.

"I'll ask you to stay here for now, Robbie," she tells me. "It will be better to first have just the sensitives in the room. I want him to feel he can speak plainly."

I shrug and concede. "If you need me, I'll be right here."

"Yes, thank you, dear. I don't think we will, but thank you."

I watch them climb the steep staircase, my aunt holding onto the railing for dear life. I position myself to catch her should she slip on the trampled-down carpet.

Chapter 19 - Sandi

The atmosphere shifts from the warm, lively bodies on the second floor to a peaceful stillness in the attic room. I welcome the creepy feelings that come with a ghost. I expect them, but you never really get used to them. I take a deep, focused breath and invite Ai to hold my hand.

"He's on my bed; do you see him?" Ai's voice is shaky. "He's standing now. He's in front of me."

"My goodness," I say as calmly as possible. "He's a tall one, isn't he?" I firmly grip Ai's hand to remind her I'm here. I'm in her corner. This translucent image of a man is barely more than a soft shadow. I'd think I hadn't put my contacts in, looking at him. It's a bit dizzying.

Ai turns to meet my gaze with a pained expression. "He's talking so fast, Sandi, I can't understand everything."

"I'm tuning into his vibration," I explain. "I'll hear him in a moment, just bear with me, dear." I allow the room to envelop me in its energy. This man is desperate to tell his story. I wait for the right vibration, and when I sense it, I hold onto it. It is a cold, wet energy that details the man's death. This is where he exists—not in the warmth of the material realm. His energy remains an unconscious reminder of where his mortal remains rest.

Suddenly, he stops jabbering at Aileen and turns his focus to me. Good. Though it's disarming. His urgency carries an intensity that chills. Ai's hand squeezes mine in return. I loosen my grip, and she responds in kind. We part ways, and I gently gesture her toward the bed with a soft point of my finger.

"Hello," I say to the ghost. "My name is Sandi, what's yours?" He looks slack-jawed now. "Cat got your tongue?" I say playfully. I suspect Ai hasn't spoken to him directly. Maybe just begged him to stop talking or to slow down. He isn't accustomed to receiving this kind of attention. "My friend mentioned you have a story to tell." I nod to Ai, sitting on her bed with her hands clasped between her knees.

"Canyouhearme?I'vesomuchtotellyou!" My goodness, that *is* fast! His words seem to come out all at once.

I nod to acknowledge the ghost, indicating that I can hear him. "Yes, but you must speak at a normal speed. We can't understand you otherwise. Can you do that? One word at a time." As he nods, he becomes even more blurry. "Good. Now, I'll ask one thing of you: to ground you further. I need you to make an impact on the material world. Be mindful of it. Concentrate on the electrical energy around you and show us you are in control of your senses."

Chapter 20 - Jesse

It's late as I stand outside the curling club, while a torrential spring rain pounds my umbrella. A nagging feeling in my gut has pulled me out of bed and forced me to take the short walk to the club. The dark puddles collecting on the asphalt shimmer and ripple. The beginning of March has been more spring-like than usual, the snow melting rapidly over the past few days. Jim Reese. The name floats in my mind, bouncing off my skull. His wife, gone. The gold medalist, gone. Yet Joe remains. Joe, who hinted at the mysteries beneath the ice. Joe. A killer. I'm sure of it.

The light above the building's door flickers and goes out. I'm reminded of a similar experience from my childhood, when we drove along country roads and the lights on the telephone poles would terminate as we neared. I thought I had somehow caused that. My energy cancelling out the light. Well, here I am, watching this phenomenon happen before me again. Maybe there is more to me than meets the eye.

I'm cold now and heading back to my apartment when I see him, a man standing in the darkened parking lot. Does he see me? How long has he been standing there, staring at the curling club? Is it him? Joe? They say the criminal always returns to the scene of the crime. He has it easy, though. He's a member, isn't he? He was at the same event I attended. But maybe, like me, he was only visiting. My hands form fists, my knuckles cracking.

He had himself situated in the far corner, steadily knocking back whiskeys that night. No one else approached him. He was alone. Was he checking in? Perhaps he did that every year during their public open house. Creepy.

The smell of worms emerging from the early spring mud catches in my nostrils. I've never enjoyed this smell. The birds will go into a frenzy once the rain slows.

I see the man's torso turn through the shadows and the rain. He's roughly half a hockey rink's distance from me, but I swear he's looking straight at me. Is this how I make others feel during my experiments? I'm frozen in place. My fight, flight, freeze, or fawn response has decided to freeze. It's uncomfortable. It's unwanted. Is he moving towards me? The wind picks up, and with it, me. I find my legs and sprint up the street, narrowly missing a car that whizzes by, soaking my jeans with a tidal wave of street water. When I turn and see that the man is out of sight, I stop. I'm no runner, and my chest heaves. I spit, bent over, hands resting on my knees.

Seriously. Am I causing these feelings of dread in others? I'm not feeling very proud of myself. I always believed that, as a social scientist, my experiments mattered more than any individual's feelings or emotional fallout over a few minutes with me. I'm unsure now, as the shoe is on the other foot.

I feared for my life just a moment ago. Jesus. That was intense. That was –

"Yer a bold one you are," a voice cuts through the sound of rain hitting the asphalt and pounding against my ears. I am startled into standing up and stunned to see Joe Reese emerging from a row of bushes along the sidewalk. "Reconsidering membership?"

I can't speak, of course. I shake my head quickly—no, my mouth a tight slash across my face. I might have whimpered. Did I? He is tall but old. I shouldn't be afraid of him, but there's something about his energy. Something dark. Darker than mine. He stares up at me, jaw clenched and eyes unblinking. He steps back, and the rain tapers off, revealing a terrifying silence.

"You didn't have much to say the other night either. You mute?"

I barely nod, a small frown creeping across my face. A cool breeze hits my damp, bare neck, sending a shiver down my spine.

"What brings you by on a night such as this? Hmm, curiosity." He tells me knowingly. "That's the only explanation. What did I tell you that night, eh? You think you know something?"

My head promptly shakes no, but I feel I've been found out. I glance at his hands tucked deep into his jacket pockets and wonder what might accompany them. A knife? A gun? A hammer? Would he prefer a blunt weapon?

"Maybe you have some questions for me, hmm? You wanna know what lies beneath the sheet, eh?" His questions are statements. I'm found out.

I swallow hard. It hurts my throat. I'm so underprepared for an encounter like this. I have no training. I'm just a big guy. I could throw a punch, but I might miss, or he could duck it and stab me or shoot me. I am at his mercy, and it is chilling.

"I guess a mute wouldn't have much in the way of questions. Do yourself a favour, kid. Leave it alone. You don't know the first thing about what happened here. Not many do. Well," dramatic pause for my benefit. "Not anymore."

Then he steps around me, nudging my arm as he goes. It feels like a warning. It *is* a warning. He'd said as much. He's warned me off his scent.

"Don't start talking now, kid!" he shouts back at me. Me, standing stock still. "There are other ways to spend your time that won't cost you so dearly."

I turn slowly after a few seconds, and he's gone. I breathe in and realize I'd been holding my breath. I bend over my knees again and breathe in, exhale, and repeat. I'm rattled to my core.

When I return to my apartment, I take a shower to warm up, unsure whether it was the rain or the frigid encounter with Joe Reese that made me so cold. Then I get dressed and sit down to write a letter to my neighbours, whom I may or may not have split up due to my careless experiment. I haven't seen either of them since that party. I need to come clean. I must ask for their forgiveness.

Chapter 21 - Rob

My aunt leans over the railing above me and whispers for me to answer the phone.

I was ignoring it, but I rounded the corner and picked up the landline. Yes, I still have a landline—something to do with my internet. It's not like I'm 'paying' for it. It's a conduit for scammers looking to collect on phony debt, offer 'free' vacation packages, or cheat me out of my Old Age Security. So, I rarely pick it up if I don't recognize the number on my digital display.

I grab the cordless phone and check the number, only to see that it's unregistered. That's a new one. I press the Talk button and hold the receiver to my ear. Nothing yet. I say, "Hello?" Still nothing. Then a burst of static jolts through the speaker. I pull the receiver away from my ear and call back to my aunt and Ai in the attic room.

"Nothing on the other end but static, guys."

"Nothing?" Aileen asks.

"Nope."

"Thank you, Robbie," my aunt replies, and I look at the receiver in my hand.

"Did you want me to hang up?" I'm unsure why there was an urgency to answer the phone and connect the dots. "Wait, is it the *ghost* calling?!" This sends a new shiver down my spine.

"We asked for a sign. I believe we received it. I'm just trying to adjust my connection. Thank you."

"Uh, okay." I hover a finger on the Talk button to hang up, pause, and ask again. "So, I should hang up?"

"Yes," both Ai and Auntie say in unison.

I press the button and keep my phone in my pocket. I peek around the opposite corner of the staircase and see my daughter actively dressing her Ken doll in a tuxedo. A series of Barbies, dressed in their Sunday best as bridesmaids for the upcoming nuptials my aunt has asked her to prepare for, line up in the background.

Above me, I hear my aunt asking questions, but I don't catch the answers. I smell candles and think I see the lights flickering on the staircase. Something is definitely happening. I feel lighter, thinking we might be rid of our ghost soon, but a sense of dread fills my chest as well, knowing it's confirmed that my house is haunted at this very moment.

Chapter 22 - Jesse

I step out of my basement apartment, letter in hand, and quickly head to the couple's home, where I have caused a rift in their marriage by planting doubt in the husband's mind through my unresponsive behaviour to his desperate questions.

I've never felt guilty about the impact of my experiments on individuals. Still, something about my meeting with Joe tonight has opened a door within me I had never considered. Could experiencing genuine fear have revealed my capacity for empathy? Am I developing feelings I thought I had lost? That's *growth*, isn't it? I haven't thought of growth outside of education. This is emotional growth. Emotional intelligence.

The butterflies thump against my sternum, and this time, I know they're not bats because the sensation is almost joyful. It doesn't share the dark humour of the bats. It is purer, perhaps even more sustainable.

I drop my letter in Jeff and Lilly's mailbox, lit beneath their porch light, and quietly slip away into the night. I'm not ready to confess my sins face-to-face.

The rain begins again. Pulling my jacket over my head, I hurry down the street to my basement suite. The screen door is slightly ajar, and the wind repeatedly slams it against the threshold. I slip inside and gently shut the door behind me. My landlords, who live upstairs, won't appreciate the banging at 11:30 at night.

I take off my jacket and hang it by the door. I towel my hair dry and return to my desk, sitting heavily with a sigh. I watch a smile light up my face in the reflection of my darkened monitor. Then, just as quickly, the smile disappears. A silhouette of a man standing behind me steps into the reflection. I turn in my seat to see Joe Reese, and I'm staring down the barrel of a gun.

"Don't make a sound," he orders in his gruff voice, so I stop the vibration rising in my throat with a squeak and swallow hard.

"Curiosity killed the cat." Joe stands behind the rickety coffee table between us, where I eat all my meals, pistol aimed at my midsection.

My guts churn. I'm afraid I'll throw up or make a sudden movement with my gag reflex that will tighten his trigger finger and end me. I slowly raise both hands in a placating gesture. My mouth has gone dry, but words won't come anyway.

"Still nothing to say? I guess I did all the talking the other night. Told you too much. Now you're heading to the club in the middle of the night looking for answers."

He sneers at me. If he's killed before, he might not hesitate to kill again to keep his secret.

"You've heard of a crime of passion?" I nod, trying to show my understanding. "Good. Because that's all it was. A crime of passion. I loved my wife."

Oh, shit. He's confessing ... to *me*. That can only mean one of two things: he'll kill me once he's finished, or he'll turn himself in. But that raises a question: who brings a gun to a confession? Maybe he just needs my full attention.

"She was a helluva curler, too." I'm getting the extended version. That means I have time to consider my escape plan.

"Best Skip I ever had the pleasure of playing with." Joe sniffs. "She was a winner. Couldn't take that away from her. You know, she played since she was wee. Almost made the Ontario championships."

Okay, is this becoming conversational? I'm not a conversationalist. He knows this. He's just unloading on me.

"We met at the university. Played for the school's team in a mixed league. Got married. No kids." He's abbreviating now. That's not good. Christ, I wish I could say something. Keep the dialogue going.

What's wrong with me? Speaking might save my life! Do I not have a survival mode? My fight, flight, freeze, or fawn response is frozen again. I'm trapped inside my own body. I feel my throat seize up as I long for words to come out. To plead for my life.

"You probably know about the Olympic team that visited our club a while back. Gold winners. Everything my wife ever wanted." Joe scratches his beard with his free hand. "She loved that. She couldn't stop talking about the planned visit for a month beforehand and then arranged the dinner and celebrations at the club for their arrival."

He's in the middle of waxing now, a glassy look in his eyes. If I could leap from my seat and wrestle the gun away from him, I would undoubtedly overpower him. I'd be a hero. I'd have solved a cold case. But here I sit, hands still raised, blinking the sweat off my invisible eyelashes as cold settles into my bones once more.

"I knew she respected the Gold Medal Skip more than she did our history. Our marriage. Our complacent love. That's all it had become. Maybe that's true for most. Love is fickle. It's not meant to last when there are other, better men to fall for."

I have a bad feeling the story is about to end. For God's sake, move—your mouth, your legs, your arms—anything!

"Yeah. So, she left me for him."

Wait. Is he saying he didn't kill her? She actually left? Then, why is his gun trained on me?

"Of course, I couldn't just let that happen. I couldn't be the loser she thought I was."

Shit.

"They didn't get very far. I found them at the club. She had the keys and the alarm codes. They were making love on the ice, if you can believe it. I watched everything from the bar, where you and I had our chat during the open house."

He's waving the gun at me now, making me part of his story. I don't want to be involved in his story. People who end up in this story die.

"It was dark inside the bar, but the lights shone below on the rink. I watched for a bit and then poured myself a few whiskeys from the bar rail. I was feeling no pain when they came up with the intention of leaving for good." Joe licks his lips as if he can taste the liquor on them.

I want to ask him why he's telling me this. Why does he need to tell me? Am I his Father confessor? Will he turn himself in after this? Or am I a dead man he knows he can unload on?

"I used a bat. The one from my summer league."

That answers my earlier question. He prefers a blunt instrument.

"First, I hit him. I wanted her to see him lose. Then I wanted her to see that *she* had lost. And I hit her. I knew enough not to keep hitting them on the bar floor. I didn't want to have to clean up a lot of blood. I didn't want a crime scene."

What he is describing isn't a crime of passion. It was deliberate. Calculated. He knew exactly what he was doing and executed the murders with a clear plan. Passion would have meant he bludgeoned the lovers to death right then and there with multiple swings of his bat until he ran out of energy and collapsed to the floor. I've seen enough TV Cop dramas to know this is true.

"I rolled their bodies in those rubber rugs that get picked up and replaced by a service every week and dragged them out of the bar." He breathes deeply and releases the breath slowly. "I took them to the ice. I defrosted a square inch of the ice on one of the sheets beyond the Hack line. Then I chipped at the concrete with my hammer and chisel. I realized I couldn't fit their bodies under the sheet. Not in one piece."

No. Don't say it.

"So, I abandoned that plan, took my wife's and Gold Medal Skip's wedding rings from their fingers, and placed them in the hole I'd managed in the concrete. I repaired the hole, filled it with water, waited for it to freeze, then used the Zamboni and scraper to finish the sheet. The bodies and their packed bags I discarded in the woods after I ... well, they weren't dead when we left the club."

Sickened and exhausted over the details, I wonder: Where will he bury my body?

Chapter 23 - Sandi

The phone call was to assign our ghost a different project from the one he's focusing on, to help him relax. I ask him to perform another task, and the light bulb in Ai's bedside lamp flickers and goes out.

"Very good," I tell him as Ai watches from behind anxious eyes. "This is good," I insist. "The more we can persuade him to listen, the easier it will be to receive his message and help him transition."

"He's pacing," Ai says, her eyes tracking the ghost.

"One more thing," I turn my attention back to our visitor. "Do you see others like you? Others who have made the shift from material to immaterial?"

"Iseenoone." He says too quickly.

"Tell me what you do see."

"You. Her. Darkness. You are both in light." I nod to Ai, who also notices that the ghost's speech has slowed.

"Good. Then be present with us. You're doing very well. We could follow along with your last statement very easily. Try to speak at that pace, no faster." My tone has not changed since entering the attic room. I remain calm, hoping that this misplaced soul matches my energy.

In response, the ghost's image has also started to become clearer. Its features and clothing are becoming more distinguishable.

Just then, a shadowy energy interrupts our connection—a troubled spirit, someone with a dark past. It is overwhelming. The ghost we've been trying to communicate with disappears. In his place is a new personality. The emotions coming through are filled with jealousy, rage, hurt, and fear—ugly feelings that cast a dark shadow over the space.

"He's gone," Ai says, startled. "Is that it? Has he crossed?"

"No," my intuition sharpens, and I picture a veil of gold settling over Ai and me. It acts as a protective bubble to shield us from whatever cruel energy has disturbed our séance.

"We've got a new visitor. A spiteful energy. We've lost our friendly ghost for now."

Ai suddenly stops and says, "I-I can't sense that." Frosty breath escapes her mouth as the temperature plummets.

"It's a spirit, not a ghost. It exists in a deeper dimension." I shiver, circle in small steps, scanning the room, looking up, down, side to side. "Why have you come?" I direct the question at the unwelcome spirit, voice cracking.

"He is mine!" the spirit's voice echoes.

"Do you hear him, Ai, the spirit?" I rub my upper arms to fight the cold.

"I don't, but why is it so cold?"

"This is a powerful spirit. It is altering the atmosphere. Its presence is demonic. Whatever it was in life multiplied in the afterlife. All its anger, hate, and malice." I raised my hand, directing Ai to be silent as I speak to the spirit who is assaulting our space.

" *Who* is yours?"

"He is mine!" The voice rumbles in my ears like a raging river.

This spirit is single-minded, focused on one task. I assume he means the ghost haunting Ai in my nephew's house. But who is *he* to him?

"He's gone now. You've missed him, and he won't be back. Leave us now and do not return." I feel shaky confronting such evil, but I adopt my momma bear tone. It's been known to scare off bullies when my kids were young.

"I will have him," the spirit insists and then disappears. Warmth returns to the attic room. Ai is standing next to me.

"This spirit. *Who* does it want?" She suddenly feels protective of her ghost – I sense it.

"Your ghost," I confirm her fears, and sit heavily on the too-low couch. "And it is hellbent on its goal."

Chapter 24 - Jesse

"I was cleared of any wrongdoing," Jim says, assuming a more casual stance, leaning his back against the basement wall. "They always suspect the partner. But, no bodies, no crime. That old chestnut.

"They call it the perfect crime." He pauses and reflects. "I'm not proud of what I did. But she wasn't a saint. She'd done something similar in the past. *Cheated.*" He says the word through tight lips and clenched teeth. "But we got through that spell. I think maybe I felt justified in acting on her betrayal the second time around."

If I survive this, my thesis on making someone open up and spill their guts will be studied in classrooms everywhere. I mean, *Jesus,* Jim is breaking down the walls he'd built and maintained for decades. I imagine the release is cathartic for him. What if being a mute psychotherapist is the right angle? Maybe I'll have invented a new form of therapy. Make your patient uncomfortable through silence and see what breaks through the barrier.

It has been my experience, and the working theory behind my dissertation, that people come to terms with their demons more openly when they have someone in front of them who is simply listening.

He seems to notice I've lost the narrative and retreated into my head.

"Am I not holding your attention?" His hand, brandishing the gun, wiggles. "You know, I followed you that night we first met. I knew I'd been too obliging with information and wanted to see where to track you down should you become ... curious."

I nod, and the tension returns to my expression. My face aches. I'm worried he has done something to my landlords and betray my thoughts by looking at the ceiling.

"No, I haven't done anything to the kindly old couple upstairs," then he jerks the gun at me again. "Not yet, at least."

He rolls his neck, and there's an audible crack. He sighs and wipes his gnarled face. The sound of a dry, rough palm dragging against his thick, grey beard scrapes at my ears.

"So, what do I do with you? Eh? You don't seem to have much in the way of fight in ya. Though you're a big lad. You a pacifist or something?"

I say nothing. I don't like him painting me as a coward, but I suppose the description is accurate. I've never fought anyone. My courage is in remaining silent in the most uncomfortable situations. It's being tested now.

"Why don't we take a walk. Try anything and I'll put you down, then I'll have to go upstairs and put that lovely couple down. Your choice." He wags the gun to his right, prompting me to get up and move to the door.

Outside, the rain has stopped. I am led down the street, Jim behind me. We pass Jeff and Lilly's house, where they sit on their front porch. They're holding hands, studying each other, sharing a cigarette. I can't hear them, but I get the feeling they've made up. This lifts my spirits. I feel happy for them. A warmth spreads through my body as the butterflies' flutter inside me. I want to call out to them, alert them to my letter in their mailbox if they haven't already found it, but that might set Jim off and drag them into my nightmare. Instead, I lower my head and feel a smile lifting my cheeks, forcing my eyes to close.

Perhaps I was the therapy they needed. Maybe I did some good.

"Something funny?" Jim asks. I must have released an ironic, euphoric hum. I didn't notice. I shake my head, no. This is my moment. This is for me.

When we reach the edge of the lake, I feel disappointed to see a patch of brush that obscures the view from the sidewalk up the bank. The sky is lit up across the lake where the city of Burlington sleeps unaware of this man's murderous intent. No one is around. The night is completely dark on the water. I am pushed into the brush and feel the coldness of death creeping over me. It starts at the back of my neck, the hairs reaching for the crescent moon, where clouds part before it, and quickly travels down my spine. A tear slips out. Will I allow myself to die this way without even a whimper? It seems pointless, but when have I ever made sense to anyone?

"On yer knees," Jim orders. Will I comply?

I decide instead to turn and face Jim. Perhaps if he addresses the will to live in my eyes, he will diverge from this course. I don't want to die. He should at least know that much. I must show *some* sign of fear and desire in my expression.

Jim chuckles as I invite him to see me. "Tell you what, say something. Anything, and maybe I'll let you go."

Bastard. He knows I can't speak. Now more than ever, I want to, but I can't. I'm terrified. I'm frozen. I open my mouth, and he waits. My jaw drops slack. I try to make a sound, but nothing crosses my vocal cords. I sigh as I close my mouth.

"This is your *life*," Jim explains. "You can't say something to save your life?"

He's toying with me like a cat with a cornered mouse. He's enjoying my suffering. I can relate. I've enjoyed others' discomfort as I conducted my experiments. Although I've never wanted or expected the finality I feel now.

"What kind of man has no voice?" he seems dismayed by this idea. "To be given a chance at life for something as simple as speaking a word." He shakes his head.

I admit it is a dreadful thing, my inability to speak when given such an opportunity. However, I doubt Jim's sincerity. I think he just wants to break me before he kills me. Still, this is an opportunity to go out on a high note. To give myself the gift of speech.

"It's a choice yer making right now, kid. You have all the power. I'm just the consequence of yer inaction."

Maybe he doesn't want to kill me. Maybe he's searching for a reason, and this request for me to speak is his way of avoiding it. So, I try harder. Jim laughs softly, dripping with irony. I try again and feel the hot wind pass my Adam's apple and exit my lips. It's not enough.

"It's not that you can't speak. It's not like you're dumb. Say something," he urges.

I can speak. I speak to my mother. I try to distance myself from the situation and imagine my mother's face replacing Jim's, but that doesn't help. I feel my forehead wrinkle and shudder. I squeak out the words that have been struggling to erupt throughout this ordeal.

"Fuck ... you," I croak, and Jim laughs louder. He is visibly taken aback by the combination of my voice and what I most wanted to convey. I feel pride. I feel everything. Was the threat of death my therapy?

"Fuck ... you ... Jim," I stuttered out a second time. This concerns him now – my knowing his name. His brow furrows and eyes light up with intention. He points the gun at me with renewed purpose.

"You know my name." His eyes narrow. "You shouldn't have said my name."

I agree, I shouldn't have, but since he's made this so personal, I felt I needed to respond in kind. I step back. The rain begins to fall again in sheets.

I feel a sensation that pushes me forward with blinding speed rather than back, and I grasp Jim's gun. It fires, and I sense a horrible heat surging through my abdomen as I wrestle the pistol out of Jim's feeble hands.

I drop backward and hit the ground hard, landing in a seated position. I turn the gun around and hold it as I've seen in the movies, finger on the trigger and firing it at my attacker. Once, twice, three times the gun goes off before I drop it between my legs.

Jim's muffled scream is lost in the driving rain, just as I imagine the gunshots are. I see him lying on his back, unmoving. Lucky shots?

I feel weak, frantically searching for the source of the heat and pain in my abdomen. Blood is indeed thicker than water. Soaked to the bone now, the entry wound is releasing its own wet, sticky essence, attaching itself to my clothing and my hands. I pull my hand to my nose to take in the metallic scent of blood. I taste it to be sure. This may seem bizarre, but until you've been shot in the dark and under a torrential rainfall, you can't know how you'll react.

Next, the pain comes. Yes, I'm in shock, but the full realization of the wound is registering. A gunshot to the belly. It's likely a mortal wound. I should stand up and seek help. I stagger to my feet and let out a long, sorrowful groan. The pain is overwhelming, and I fall to my knees, one hand pressing against the hole in my guts while the other keeps me up. I crawl past Jim's lifeless body to the sidewalk above us and collapse. I roll onto my back and open my mouth thirstily to the sky, letting the renewed rainfall land on my tongue. I hear myself cry for help before I lose consciousness.

Chapter 25 - Rob

"You can come up, Rob," I hear my aunt call down from the attic room.

I leave my daughter and climb the steep stairs, finding Ai seated on her bed and my aunt absorbed in the plush, second-hand couch.

"How did it go? Did you make contact or whatever?" My eyes dart from one to the other, searching their expressions for an answer.

My aunt struggles to get off the couch, and I hurry to help, letting her pull herself out by grabbing my forearm. She lets out a tight yelp, and when she stands, she palms her lower back.

"Thank you, dear," she says, glancing back at the infernal chesterfield. "We did make contact, yes," she reflexively looks to Ai. "More than we'd bargained for, I fear."

"How do you mean?" My stomach drops. I sense a dark cloud descending over my aunt's face, gently shaping her soft features into a frown. A very unnatural expression for her.

"We encountered Ai's ghost, but we also encountered something more ... diabolical."

"Diabolical!" I announce, then whisper/scream, "Like, a demon?"

"Dark, but I'm not sure we encountered a demon. An evil, yes. But one, I believe, that originated in our world."

"Another ghost then," I surmise, though I admit I am out of my depth here.

"Reminds me of a story," my aunt tells us, taking a seat next to Ai on the much higher, less plush bed.

I'm excited to hear what my aunt will tell us, as I've always loved listening to her ghost stories. I plunk myself on the couch, pulling a throw pillow onto my lap.

"Your uncle and I were in Savannah, Georgia, exploring an area where there was a beautifully detailed monument of an African American family, marking one of the places where slaves were once sold.

"I pictured the families being separated as they often were, and felt an immense sadness. I began to cry as if it were happening to me." She looks up, and I see tears teetering in her eyes now.

"Empaths," she states with a sad laugh. "Time does not lessen the energies that surround a place with that kind of history, that level of cruelty attached to it, and someone like me will sense that energy. It was a devastating feeling."

"And you felt similar emotions tonight?" Ai asks softly, gently resting a calming hand on my aunt's upper arm. My aunt places her hand over Ai's and nods.

"Similar in that your ghost was distraught, terrified, and violently separated from this life. Torn from his reality and thrown into a new, unfamiliar, and frightening one." My aunt pulls a tissue from the pocket of her cardigan and dabs her nose.

"But that's not all I felt. The other ghost, the wicked one, seemed entitled, like those slavers might have felt. He was angry. He felt cheated and wanted your ghost to suffer with him for what, I sensed, he had caused."

"He wants to own the other ghost," I say, gripping the pillow in my lap, hairs dancing on the back of my neck.

"In a sense, yes." She looks at Ai again. "But we're not going to let that happen, are we?" Ai shakes her head, bottom lip exposed.

"He's a nice ghost, my ghost," Ai explains with a curt nod. "I believe he is, like your aunt says, scared. Confused."

"He just wants to tell us his story, and then he'll go to the light. Once he's gone, the other should vanish too." My aunt's eyes darken, carrying a warning with them if they can't convince Ai's ghost to make the transition. "The evil spirit will only haunt this place if our ghost is present."

"Then we need to get him back, the *good* ghost, hear his story, and put an end to this," I conclude, leaning forward. A ghost is one thing; an evil spirit is something else entirely. I have my daughter with me half the time. I won't let this thing near her. Both women nod. "So, how do we do that?"

Chapter 26 - Sandi

We take a break for the night, and I tell Ai that if she senses any ghosts again tonight, she can wake me up in the guest room in my nephew's basement.

Rob and I enjoy tea in his living room after an hour of playing with Katie. He's left the television off as calming music fills the silence.

"It's one of the albums I play for my clients," he tells me, noticing how I've begun to sway to the melody. "Promotes a peaceful experience."

"Mmmm," I hum. "That's the idea, I suppose." I sip the hot, herbal tea. I take this moment to unwind from the evening's events. Inhaling the peppermint steam and listening to soft music creates a perfect blend.

"Katie really enjoyed spending time with you today," he tells me. "She loves your energy." I'm so glad to hear it.

"Your daughter is a doll, Robbie." I see the kid I knew in him, looking into his caramel-coloured eyes now. "She reminds me of your cousin, Mindy. I wonder if Katie, too, will show similar signs of her lineage."

"You know, I've asked her about that casually. I don't want to push it. But I also asked her about her past life a few months ago. I understand that children under four still have access to their previous lives." I'm surprised he hasn't told me this yet.

"Oh, that's interesting," I shift in my seat to face him. "Yes, children often have that silver umbilical that keeps them grounded to their past. It's only when the material world truly becomes their focus that the magic disappears."

"She told me that she was once yellow. That she was called *Big Mumma*," Rob laughs at the memory. "She said she ate a lot of bananas."

"Isn't that fascinating. I wonder what she meant by it." I take another sip, my gaze remaining on Robbie's, drifting past the oversized cup, tilting toward my mouth.

"Yeah, it could be anything. I thought maybe she was from South America or somewhere like that. A place where bananas are common. She told me she had a big family. But that was about it," he sips his tea. "She might have picked that up from a TV show, though."

"Oh, I wouldn't bet on that," I say, placing my cup on the coffee table. "Katie might well have been accessing the ether at the time. It's a fascinating topic, past lives."

Rob places his cup next to mine and addresses the evening's events. "So, what's the plan for our ghosts? Do we need a plan? Will they just show up again?"

"Since Ai's ghost has been visiting repeatedly, I feel confident he will return. Though I worry the dark entity has given him pause."

"So, best to just wait it out? Will you stay with us until we convince him to go to the light?"

"Yes, I'll run home in the morning, pack a bag, visit your uncle at hospice, and come straight back." My tone carries an intensity that I hope is reassuring.

Next, a scrambling down the stairs interrupts our quiet conversation. Ai appears around the corner, finding Rob and I on the couch opposite the fireplace.

"He's back," I announce before Ai has the chance. She nods quickly, and I see the urgency in her face. I stand up.

"He's confused again," Ai says, her face scrunching up. "Can you come, please?"

I look at Rob and stop him with calming hands. "Stay put, Rob, maybe bring Katie down and let her sleep on the couch tonight. It could get noisy."

With that, I follow Ai in her flowing pyjamas up the two flights of stairs. Our ghost is blurry and pacing in her attic room, but he stops once he senses me entering.

I focus on matching his energy. I need more information about him. I need a deeper connection to resolve his issues. I need ... "Your *name*," I whisper emphatically. "Tell us your name."

Chapter 27 - Jesse

I know I'm rambling, but once the older woman appears where I first found the younger woman, who can hear and see me, I feel more at ease. I quickly go to her, and she asks my name.

"Jesse," I tell her, trying to remember to speak slowly, as she'd requested the last time we met. This is new territory for me. I've never really spoken before. Certainly not like this. But somehow, I've lost any hesitation to communicate.

"Jesse," the older lady repeats, glancing at the young woman whose space I've been invading for the past ... I don't know how long. Time has lost all meaning to me since the incident with Jim. I don't even know how I got here, if not for the aura that surrounds her. She's like a beacon in the night.

"Jesse, why are you here?" The older lady asks in a gentle tone. Her aura matches that of the younger ones', but is somehow more structured and substantial.

I want to focus on my words, but first need to ask both women, *"Isthisadream?"*

They share an unsettling look.

"Let's start with our names, Jesse. I'm Sandi, and this is Ai. Aileen cannot understand much of what you say when you speak so fast. English is not her first language."

"I'm sorry, I want to understand what is happening to me."

"Good, Jesse, that's much better when you speak slower like that. To answer your question, no, this is not a dream. You are experiencing a stage of the afterlife." Sandi's revelation terrifies me.

"You mean I'm ... dead?"

"I don't know of any other explanation, Jesse."

"Then he did manage to kill me," I say almost to myself. A heavy feeling drops me to my knees. "I thought I might have been saved. That this was all a dream."

"I'm so sorry," the young one, Ai, says in a comforting tone. Both women stand over me, or the spectral me, or whatever I've become.

"Wait, then, I'm a ghost?" Shouldn't they be terrified of me then?

"You are, dear," Sandi confirms in her soft tones. "We can see and speak with ghosts, and that is why you were drawn to Ai."

"Because I have unfinished business to pass on."

"Yes. Do you want to tell us now?"

I gather myself off the floor and pace among the women. I honestly thought I might just be dreaming all of this. The notion of having died and my consciousness surviving in this dreamlike state feels more surreal than if I were dreaming. I gather my thoughts and continue with my story.

"I was murdered. But I don't know if the man who murdered me was himself killed. I wrestled his gun away from him after he'd fired on me. Then I shot him. He went down."

If I could feel anything beyond emotions, I know my forehead would be sore from pulling my brows tightly together as I recall the incident. My concentration is intense.

"I staggered up the embankment to a sidewalk or pathway, where the rain had become torrential. I thought I would be found and saved. It was dark, and I didn't know the city well where he took me. By the lakeside. A Bayfront something. Park? They have events there, I think. I've never been."

Sandi makes a move as if to comfort me with her hands, then realizes that is not an option. "A violent death is often met with disbelief," she explains. "Which, in turn, works against the individual from moving into the light."

"I did move into the light," I say, *"I moved toward Ai. She was my light."*

"I mean, on to the next chapter," Sandi says sadly. "But because you have unfinished business, perhaps Ai's light is your next chapter before moving on."

"His name is Jim Reese. He lives in Hamilton. Are we in Hamilton?"

"Yes," Ai answers. "Jim shot you?"

"Exactly, he shot me for what I had discovered," I explained the curling rink, Jim's wife, the gold medalist, the double homicide, the buried bodies, and the buried rings.

"Cold cases," Sandi states. "That will be a relief for the families. I will certainly tell the police what you've told us, Jesse. I'll be sure to let them know you shot that man in self-defence. That you're the reason we have this information. Is there anything else?"

"I'd like to know if Jim survived. I don't feel good about killing someone. I was just starting to feel things. In life, I couldn't feel much. I was turned off. I didn't speak, but in those last few hours before ... I was beginning to understand what it meant to be alive, what it means to be part of something bigger than myself."

I almost can't believe I'm experiencing this. I'm a fucking ghost! I'm dead. No more me. No more experiments. No more papers to write. No more future. It's devastating. My parents will be distraught. My professors. My work will be forgotten. I was so excited to put it into practice someday. To have patients of my own.

To solve their problems. To have a conversation with my father. All gone.

Then darkness descends upon the women. They hold hands, and Sandi says something that sounds ancient. Is it Latin?

Chapter 28 - Sandi

"Tuere me a malo," I speak loudly and confidently, asserting my command over the situation as an unearthly darkness encroaches on the attic room. Though I'm not a religious person per se, I have found some success with the Latin phrase to 'drive away evil from me.'

Latin is an ancient language, and those who understand it on the other side are at least as old. Whatever this dark presence is, invading our space, will appreciate that I am fluent in a tongue they fear.

"Libera me a malo," I say, watching the darkness shudder. Then the voice we'd heard before returns.

"He's mine," it demands in a cruel tone that makes me cringe. The walls emit a creaking as if they are straining to contain this malevolent energy. The smell of sulphur penetrates the space.

I glance at Jesse, who has stepped between Ai and me. He turns to me and asks, "W-what is that?"

Ai wears a similar expression of terror, her hands rubbing her upper arms to shield herself from the cold air that accompanies the darkness. I see her breath escape her lips as I did the first time this wicked spirit entered here. This is a powerful entity. I hesitate to call it a demon, as I tend to separate the supernatural from religious terminology. I'm no priest, and I don't believe I have God on my side.

"It is an evil that seems to have attached itself to you, or the idea of you, Jesse. I've only experienced this twice in my readings with others. It is not to be feared, only its efforts thwarted." I say this as my knees begin to shake.

"How do we stop it?" Ai asks, eyes blazing with terror.

"We go on the attack," I explain, watching the darkness redouble its efforts. "Sicut déficit fumus defíciant; sicut fluit cera a fácie ígnis, sic péreant peccatóres a fácie Dei."

What I say is part of an exorcism prayer. Yes, it is from the Catholic canon, but it has been effective in past attempts to repel an evil intrusion during a reading. I repeat it in English to encourage Ai and Jesse to say it with me.

"As smoke vanisheth, so let them vanish away: as wax melteth before the fire, so let the wicked perish at the presence of God.

"Say it with me," I tell them, and take Ai's outstretched hand. It's as cold as ice. I repeat the verse three times, and they follow my lead.

The darkness starts to lift as we keep chanting. I can only imagine what Robbie must think if he can hear us two floors below, where I asked him to take Katie.

"He's mine, wicked bitch!" the unholy voice threatens. *"I will take you all if you do not release him."*

"You have no power here," I shout, not quite as convincingly as I'd meant. No doubt in my mind that Rob heard that. "Leave us!"

A wind has entered the attic room's atmosphere, whipping Ai's curtains about and tearing off her bedsheets. Papers from her desk leap into the swirling mess, and I duck to avoid them.

Whatever this entity is, it has decided to show us how mistaken I was to claim it powerless.

"This boy is mine!" it screams. I am unsure whether its cries are audible only to us three or if Robbie and Katie can also hear them. My body shudders at the screeching.

Ai's long hair is thrown around her face and begins to wrap around her throat. Her grip on my hand tightens as her hair forms a noose around her long neck. Then she lets go of my hand and pulls at her animated hair.

"I will take the girl, then," the voice insists with malicious delight.

I realize I will have to pull out the big guns and say, "Exsúrgat Deus et dissipéntur inimíci ejus: et fúgiant qui odérunt eum a fácie ejus!" Meaning, Let God arise and let

His enemies be scattered: and let them that hate Him flee from before His Face!

With this, I fervently remove the crucifix I keep in my purse. My outstretched arm bends at an unnatural angle, testing the strength of my conviction.

"Écce Crúcem Dómini, fúgite pártes advérsae!" Meaning, Behold the Cross of the Lord, flee away ye hostile forces!

With my free hand, I help Ai remove her hair that's snaking around her throat.

"Your words hold no power over me, old woman!" the entity spits. *"Neither does your crucifix."*

I wrestle the hair from Ai's throat and consider what the voice just claimed. I need this entity's name. If I know its name, as is common with evil spirits, it should become more susceptible to suggestion. I might gain the upper hand.

"What are you?" I ask, Ai's hair in my hand, writhing against me. "Robbie!" I yell down the stairs, realizing I'm not going to be able to help Ai and Jesse on my own. "Get up here!"

Chapter 29 - Rob

In the family room, Katie is fast asleep, wrapped in her princess blanket on the floor, surrounded by half a dozen stuffed animals. Jackson lies beside her when, suddenly, his ears perk up at the sound of my aunt's frantic cry for me to join them in the attic.

I share a glance with Jackson and gesture for him to stay. He's a good boy and understands his role is to protect Katie while I answer the call. He circles her once, a low growl rumbling from his throat, and then lies down again with his head resting on her legs. I rush up the stairs.

In Ai's room, it smells like a sewer, papers swirl around the ceiling, and the air has cooled significantly. "Oh, this can't be good," I say, swatting at the windstorm. I find my aunt and Ai and hurry to take my aunt's place in removing the hair that is threatening to choke Ai.

"What are you?!" my aunt shouts, staring at nothing in particular. At least, it's nothing my limited senses can identify as something one would talk to.

"*I am what he made me!*" a demonic voice answers. I'm riddled with bone-chilling shivers at the sound.

My aunt turns to look at another invisible personality and asks, "What did you say your murderer's name was?" She nods as if someone had responded.

"Jim Reese, you will leave this house," she commands the other invisible entity in an authoritative tone that recalls my youth.

"*He did this to me!*"

"You did this to yourself!" My aunt isn't buying what this Jim Reese character is telling her. She drops the crucifix and steps closer to where I imagine Jim must be. I rush to pick it up. Just in case.

"You will answer for your crimes in the next life," she insists. "Leave Jesse and this house forever."

"*I won't. He's mine.*" The voice sounds less sure now. I think my aunt is gaining the upper hand.

"You will," she demands of the entity, pulling a small vial from her sweater pocket and spraying an effervescent oil into the air. I assume the ghost is of the non-biblical sort after seeing her drop the cross I now hold in both hands, Ai's hair no longer looking for purchase around her delicate throat. This is a spirit with remarkable energy for sure. To be able to manipulate so much in the real world is considerable, or so I have learned.

Ai relaxes and collapses onto her bed, having tied her hair back into a ponytail. "You're alright?" I ask her, breathless. She nods. I turn to my aunt and take her hand firmly in mine. She looks at me and nods, knowingly. I'm offering my strength to this fight.

"Where is our ghost? Can't he help?" I know he can cool a room and nudge a person, based on my earlier experience with him.

She turns her attention to another empty part of the room.

"Jesse," she whispers. "Can you do me a favour? Can you concentrate on Jim's other victims? Can you call to them?"

Chapter 30 - Jesse

Sandi is asking me to summon Jim's dead wife and her equally dead gold medalist. I don't know how to do something like that. *"How would I do something like that?"*

"Concentrate on their energies," she says, as if I have a clue.

"I don't understand," I reply anxiously. *"I never knew them."*

"But you know *of* them and share a commonality," she persists. "You're all victims of Jim's cruelty. If they remain in our realm, as you do, they will recognize this and come to you."

Next, I feel a tug on my ethereal self. It's like I'm being grabbed by my clothing and pulled toward the Jim entity, a dark cloud of vindictive energy. *"H-he's pulling me towards him,"* I tell Sandi, who is now holding the hand of a man in his late thirties. Their light has increased as a result of joining hands. Then Ai, the young Japanese woman, takes the man's other hand, and their light expands, pulsating. I can no longer distinguish them as individuals. Their combined energies have blurred the lines between them. I wonder if they can see this. It's beautiful, but I have bigger concerns. The tug at my ethereal clothing has increased, filling me with anxious energy.

"Focus on us, Jesse," she cautions me. "Use our energy to stand against him."

How can I fulfill both requests simultaneously? I wish there were a playbook on how-to-summon-the-deceased-for-the-deceased and how to utilize the energy of the living to counter the impossible pull of another ghost. But, unfortunately, I have not received such a playbook.

"I really don't know how to do that," I tell her, now frantic over the progress Jim is making against me. What is he doing? Is he going to claim my immortal soul? Is that possible? Can a ghost be taken prisoner?

"Focus on our light," she explains. "Join our light. If you're within our protective light, he can not take you." Next, she scrambles for something more in her sweater pocket. Salt? She sprinkles it around the three of them.

So, I attempt to do my part and concentrate. It's hard because I feel like I'm being pulled to hell or something, but the brightness they emit is so intense that I can focus long enough to enter their safe space, and the pull diminishes.

"Go, now, Jim Reese, and do not come back. You are not welcome here. You have no control over Jesse.

You are powerless in this place!" Sandi shouts convincingly. I immediately feel grateful for her presence.

I watch as the papers twirl through the atmosphere, fluttering and dropping around us while Jim's negative energy field disintegrates, and he disappears.

"You did it," Ai says. The three release each other's hands, the light returning to their individual, healthy bodies.

"Thank you," I say, focusing on Ai and Sandi. Rob can't see me, so it seems pointless to make eye contact with him.

"You did well, Jesse," Sandi says to me, breathless. "The name was crucial in gaining dominance over him. You followed directions." She says, and I feel proud. Sandi guides the other two to the far corner.

"I want to perform a smudging, Robbie," she tells her nephew. "Could you get my bag from the couch?" He does so, and she pulls out a large ... what looks like a massive joint, reminiscent of my time at some of the wilder college parties, poorly rolled with a string holding it together.

"Smudging with sage will help cleanse the space of Jim's negative energies." She lights it and moves around the room. Oddly, I can taste and smell this. Perhaps being a good ghost, whatever sage is supposed to do, has no adverse effects on me.

Chapter 31 - Rob

Auntie lowers herself beside Aileen on the bed, brushes the hair from her forehead and sighs heavily. "You know," she begins, blowing a stray curl from her eyebrow, and if I know one thing about my Auntie Sandi, she's about to launch into a story.

"That energy reminds me of a séance that went off the rails twenty-odd years ago." She eyes both Aileen and me, takes a breath and straightens the loose sweater secured over her heavy gingham nighty.

I sit on the low couch and prepare for the tale. Rarely has she shared one of her seances with me. Client confidentiality or some such.

"Malevolent spirits like Jim are truly frightening. Unhinged. Unpredictable," she looks to me with a sympathetic smile. "I don't mean to scare you, Robbie. We will remove him soon enough," and she winks.

"These spirits can breach the supernatural barrier and influence the natural world, which in and of itself is a terrifying concept. But it is one I am familiar with. One I'd experienced once before, when I was in my fifties, holding seances in my home." She rubs her hands together as if to remove the stain of the memory.

"I would send my husband out to the movies with the kids during these sessions," she adds the disclaimer, looking to Aileen. "This story involves a séance I held for a family who had lost their youngest in an accident, depriving them of a proper goodbye. The driver of the car also died in that crash. The parents had learned that the driver had been under the influence, swerved into their daughter as she biked along the street. Then he crashed into a telephone pole, was ejected from the vehicle, and died." She shifts on the bed, toying with the vial of oil in her hand, brows crinkled together in remembrance.

"Of course, I was not privy to this information before I began the séance. It was revealed only after the daughter accepted my invitation to be her medium. The reunion was emotional and provided a sense of closure for her family. Her parents and siblings were pleased with the experience, and as I was disconnecting from the girl's ghost, I sensed a nasty, sticky, dark energy vying for control of me.

"The family hurried away while my body trembled as I fought off the spirit. I heard myself recite a few incantations I had memorized, struggling to regain control of my muscles. Then it spoke clearly and viciously, telling me it was not going back!

"'What do you mean?' I asked, struggling to swallow as the malicious spirit fought to gain power over my senses. My head tilted upward, eyes unfocused, hands gripping the armrests of the dining room chair, nails piercing the fabric." Auntie's hands form fists now, pulling at Ai's comforter.

"'Not going back,' it barked out of me."

My aunt pauses; the story obviously stirring up difficult memories. We wait for her to regain her composure.

"I reached for the bowl of salt among my baubles on the table, head still tilted upward and poured it with a shaky hand in a circle around myself. Once the circle was complete, the spirit was forced out of me and into the piano across the room with a loud bang, striking what I remembered to be the Devil's interval, an augmented fourth on the piano strings."

My aunt once taught piano, I recall.

"Then, it went wild, banging out a tritone of six semitones. A sound once avoided in ecclesiastical music for its sinister mood.

"I worked to steady myself on shaky knees and stood with my cup of oil, quickly anointing the piano with it and dedicating it to the Lord, effectively trapping the spirit within.

"It kept pounding out G7 in the key of C, causing a clash in the piece. It became manic. It was the first and only time I've experienced music originating from the supernatural realm. It was simultaneously eerie and extraordinary. I consider myself fortunate to have experienced it."

"What happened to the piano? I remember that piano," I say, visualizing it, wishing she had recorded that bit of music. "It was in your living room, with the deep scar on one side." My aunt nods.

"Right, Robbie. The piano was an heirloom from my mother. I had it quickly removed from my home, along with the spirit who was occupying it, who, I believe, was the man responsible for the death of the young girl I had channelled that night."

"So he was claiming you like Jim is claiming Jesse," Ai says. My aunt nods again, her expression changing. The exhaustion of a moment ago is replaced with renewed energy.

Chapter 32 - Sandi

I suggest we settle into Robbie's backyard to further cleanse ourselves of Jim's unwelcome energy. The fresh air feels good on my skin and in my lungs. I take several deep inhales, visualizing a white light entering my body, and carefully, mindfully releasing them, imagining darkness leaving through my breath. I encourage the others to do the same.

Robbie has brought Katie out, wrapped in a blanket, and set her on the L-shaped couch on the porch overlooking his pool.

Jesse has also followed us outside. I intuit that he does not want to be alone and empathize with him.

I feel that at this late hour, another, less intense story will further settle everyone's nerves and prepare us for bed. So, I search my memory for something familiar, something relatable to, but lighter than the energies we faced tonight. I land on a story that will connect to the sudden, frigid temperatures we experienced.

"You know, when I felt Jim's presence tonight, I immediately remembered the first time I experienced such a bone-chilling cold," I tell Robbie, Ai, and Jesse.

"Tell us, Auntie," Robbie says, the moonlight twinkling in his eyes. He appears as a younger version of himself, settling in to listen to one of my ghost stories.

"I was in Italy, specifically in Florence, on a high school trip with my peers when a man collapsed on the cobblestone in front of the Duomo. The people on the tour I was with were startled, and our guide hurried to the man with a bottle of water.

"It was a scorching day, and even the pigeons stayed out of the Piazza, remaining in the shade of the buildings. Water seemed like the right choice, as we believed the poor man had collapsed from dehydration, as many do in such heat."

"Was he dehydrated?" Ai asks, concern flickering across her fine features.

"No, he'd apparently suffered a heart attack, right there in front of the Duomo. That was later relayed to us by the paramedics."

"Your group stayed with him until they came?" Robbie wonders.

"Most, yes. Our tour guide suggested that we all go into the church to cool off if nothing else, but being mainly Canadians in the group, we stayed." I notice that I'm wringing my hands, and pause to wipe my wet palms on my cardigan.

"A moment later, a rush of cold washed over me. It wasn't a breeze; I was sure of that. It was an unnatural cold, you know? Like an air conditioner had suddenly been turned to high. I was struck by a shiver, noticing that no one else was experiencing a similar sensation."

"It was the spirit of the dead man," Ai suggests. I shake off the memory and sigh.

"Yes, and even though I was just seventeen, I knew that instinctively. He had passed right through me while crossing to the other side."

"And what's on the other side?" Robbie is perched at the edge of his seat on the couch like he had been in Ai's room. He has a history of asking this question, hoping that I will provide a more satisfactory answer each time.

"Oh, well, that's still up for debate, dear," I begin impartially. "Jesse," I motion toward his energy, "is an earthbound, interactive personality. Jim, though tragically different in energy, is also earthbound - I might even class him as a Poltergeist, or noisy ghost, after his display tonight.

"Whereas the man I saw pass away in Florence was neither of these. His spirit was resolute. He went straight to the light."

"Are there other types?" Robbie's interest is peaking.

"Certainly, there are residual ghosts, those who repeat their last action over and over. Energy caught up in a loop, so to speak. You can't carry on a conversation with them. They are unconscious. They are just a memory of the person.

"There are orbs, funnel ghosts, mist ghosts, inanimate ghosts -"

"Wait, like a ghost trapped in an object? Like a rocking chair that rocks by itself?" Robbie is enjoying this, I can tell.

"Yes, exactly like that. Similar to my Piano story. It's the energy of a deceased person, which is forever attached to an object. I have used such items to understand a person's passing in my work. The object relays the story rather than a ghost, such as Jesse." I nod again at Jesse's energy, and he acknowledges me with an awkward smile.

"What about animals?" Robbie asks, petting Jackson's soft fur on top of his head.

"Yes, indeed, animals, especially pets, can revisit their homes and owners. I have a story about my dog Max if you'd like to hear it."

"Yes, please," Ai insists before Robbie can. I chuckle at this and feel the energy around us lighten. Stories like these will help everyone unwind before bed. Harmless ghosts who want nothing of the material world.

"Well, my darling Max, he was a standard poodle, died while I was sleeping." I take a brief moment to remember him. I loved him so much. He was our last family pet.

"I woke in the night and watched my ceiling swirling in a dark, foggy smoke. Max's face emerged from the fog to me, and he barked in that subtle way he always did to get my attention. Then he was gone.

"Another instance of Max's energy was when my friend saw him in the hallway of my house while we sat in my office with the door open. I had my back to the hallway, but felt a friendly energy rush past. Shirley looked perplexed by what she'd seen. She got up, went to the hallway, and immediately stepped back as if to avoid something moving quickly through it. Shirley looked at me with a hand covering her heart." I giggle recalling the moment.

"At that time, I was used to Max showing up, and I explained to her that it was my dog. He used to love running back and forth along the hall. The zoomies, they call it." I smile at Jackson, whose head rests on Robbie's lap.

"That's a new one for me, Auntie," Robbie says, clearly enticed by the possibility. He bends down to kiss Jackson's head.

"I think we should get some sleep now, I tell them. I don't expect Jim to return tonight; he's been heavily reprimanded and is probably exhausted. I know I am. I stand and smile at them. I'll go home, Robbie, and I'll come back tomorrow after I visit your uncle."

"So - this house is clean?" Robbie teases, quoting the iconic spiritual cleanser from the movie Poltergeist. I laugh at this.

"It should provide everyone with a good night's sleep, at least. Ai, I recommend you sleep in the family room, just to be safe. Jesse, I'd like you to consider staying put and watching over everyone."

"I can do that," Jesse says, wringing his hands.

"I have every confidence in you, dear," I tell him.

Chapter 33 - Jesse

So, this whole thing about me being a ghost ... it doesn't sit right with me. Maybe that's a given, but I don't feel any pull to move on. I mean, they know my story now. Shouldn't that be enough?

Jim is one scary son of a bitch, too. He was scary in life, but in death ... he's off the charts. I don't want to deal with him again. I don't want to deal with being dead anymore. Why can't I move on?

I'll ask Sandi if she can give me a push. If I'm dead, I'm dead. It's cruel to be left to linger.

The house slips into a restless sleep, and I stay with Katie, who now shares her father's bed with the family dog. Her glow resembles a warm campfire. She has a faint silvery cord attached to her stomach.

Is she still tethered to the other side? This experience is extraordinary, I admit. I wonder if it will be remembered when I cross over.

I feel so disconnected from the material world. I can't touch anything. I did experience a burst of energy when I pushed Rob that night, but I don't know how I managed to break through the barrier between here and there. I feel I ought to be hungry. I feel I should want to use the bathroom. I should be thirsty. But none of those things matter here.

Should I attempt to conjure the Reese woman and her lover as Sandi suggested during our battle against Jim's malicious presence? Would they be reachable?

Sandi said they shared a similar fate to mine at the hands of the same man, and so perhaps there is a connection. Maybe they, too, are trying to get their story out and be vindicated.

I want to try. I focus on the photos of Carly Reese that I saw in the articles. I also picture the gold medalist and reread the announcements of their disappearances in my mind. I'd love it if they could join us to fend off Jim's efforts to abscond with my immortal soul. I'd like to remain a free spirit at least, so to speak. But what if he's already imprisoned theirs?

Nothing. They've probably left this dimension or whatever this is to be together for eternity. I can't blame them. This feels like purgatory. One foot in the world and the rest of me in the afterlife.

I consider my parents again. My mom will be inconsolable. My father probably saw this coming and prepared himself for the fallout.

I wonder where they'll bury me. Or will they cremate my remains and perhaps press them into a black diamond? Something my mom can wear to remind her that I was there. I never gave a preference. Who, at a young age, does?

I hope they don't discover the paper I've been writing in my rented apartment. It's unfair that I was so clinical and detached from those I experimented on. I feel ashamed of it. The irony of dying and being permitted to grow posthumously isn't lost on me. I couldn't seem to look beyond the dispassionate, calculating train of thought in life. Maybe there's hope for me yet.

Of course, there is no *me*, not in the physical world. Not anymore. So, if this is it, then I suppose it's better late than never to gain a new perspective on life and, perhaps, even develop a little empathy.

I think back to my death scene. I remember the place and am instantly transported to the spot where I once lay dying, as the late winter's early spring crescent moon's warmth attempted to part the wet clouds.

I move down the embankment away from the sidewalk and toward the brush where Jim shot me, and I him. I say move because, as much as my legs feel like they must be what's carrying me, I am merely floating. What's that called? A phantom sensation? Like when someone loses an arm or leg, but the impression that you still have the appendage remains. That's what it feels like to be a ghost.

There is no police tape flapping in the wind where I was murdered, tied off to the bench, trees, or other surfaces that might support a yellow "CAUTION, CRIME SCENE" tape. I wonder how long ago it was that Jim and

I acted out our final scene here. Is the brush fuller? Was that bench always there?

It's dark, just like that night. It's not raining, though, and I can feel a breeze from the lake. Funny how I can actually *feel* anything. I retrace my final, desperate trek from the brush up the short hill and to the sidewalk, where I lie down, hoping help will come. I suppose no help did come. I died in the rain, beneath the cover of clouds, far enough removed from downtown where the night owls might stumble upon me.

My bad luck, I suppose. Jim's too. I should have fought him harder and sooner. I should never have let him take me this far. It would have been better to fight him off during the walk—anywhere but in this secluded spot. Is this where he buried his wife and her lover? Hardly the woods Jim had confessed to dumping their bodies in. There isn't enough foliage in Bayfront Park to call it a forest. But, if this was Jim's preferred place to dump bodies, perhaps the police eventually excavated the area for clues and found their skeletons?

Is that why I can't conjure their ghosts?

Chapter 34 - Rob

The next day, my aunt returns to my house at 4:15 pm with Katie in tow. I'd asked her to pick her up enroute here from her mother's. It may seem an odd choice, but I want Katie close with all of this going on.

"How's Uncle?" I ask as I lay out a colouring book for Katie on the kitchen island.

"Oh, he's tired, dear," she replies, a sense of defeat in her eyes. "He asked after you."

"Have you told him about our ghost?"

"Yes, he loves my stories as much as you do, I think," she says, sits next to Katie, and picks up a crayon.

"Ai will be home soon. Is, uh, Jesse still here?" I wonder, looking around the room as if I might sense him.

"I don't see him," she tells me. "He seems to slip away occasionally. I'm not sure why, but he has travelled to be here with you and Aileen, so perhaps he wanders."

"Hey, what's he look like, anyway?"

"Oh, well, he's tall, certainly. As tall as you, I would say. He's very washed out, of course, he *is* a ghost," she explains with a smirk. "He has broad shoulders and appears to be in good shape. I can't tell the colour of his hair, but he's Caucasian. Small nose and broad mouth. Due to his faint eyebrows, I'd hazard a guess he's a redhead or albino."

"So, okay – that's pretty descriptive."

"There's something about him, though," my aunt starts, "something about his ghost that perplexes me."

"How so?"

"It's just a feeling. Something is missing."

This is beyond my pay grade. I ask, "So, we're going to help him solve his case, right? Do we have his last name?"

"Oh, no, we don't! I think after all the kerfuffle of last night, we never got back to the reason he's here. And then your old auntie went off on you all about my Max's ghost." She hugs Katie as she says this.

"Who's Max?" Katie asks, eyes like saucers.

"Oh, well, Max was my dog, Katie. He was a wonderful companion to your great-uncle and me. Very protective of us. Then, like most pets do, he died."

"Jackson will die one day," Katie explains matter-of-factly, head down, crayon moving across the page.

"Yes, he will one day. But let's hope that's a long way off," my aunt is so good with kids. Katie nods and chews her cheek as her crayon presses harder into the paper.

"When you see Jesse again, ask for his full name, and I can search for him online in archived obituaries." Saying the words aloud, I realize just how strange a thing it is we're experiencing.

I have a deceased man in my house who was murdered by this evil Jim character, whose ghost is more like a Poltergeist, and we're trying to solve the murder so the kid can move on, Ai can get back to her life, and Jim can fuck off.

"Wait," I say, "we have Jim Reese's full name and he's dead! Why don't I look him up right now?"

"That's - ha! That's funny, Robbie. I can't believe that went right over our heads!" My Aunt Sandi is beside herself, hand at her forehead, mouth agape. Head rocking back and forth. "Maybe I'll check myself into the hospice."

I laugh. "Well, we all missed it," I console her as I pull my phone out of my pocket. "Let's have a look."

I search Hamilton obituaries and enter Jim Reese. Nothing shows up for 2025. I try James Reese. Still nothing. "What the -"

"What is it, Robbie?"

"I'm not finding any hits on the obituaries for Jim Reese in the city." I'm puzzled. "Jesse said he was from Hamilton, right? Did he say?"

"I don't recall, dear," my aunt says, a mystified expression crosses over her soft features. "I guess we assumed ... and you know what that means. We've made an ASS -"

"- Out of U and ME," I finish with a tired chuckle. "Okay, I can punch the name into the regular search engine and see what we see." I do this and place *Obituaries* after it. Now I have too many search results. This is going to take forever.

Chapter 35 - Sandi

Robbie, Katie, and I eat dinner in the backyard with Aileen. It's a shared supper among us—a sort of breaking of the bread before we return to the attic.

"There's no guarantee Jesse is coming back," I tell them, "But I suspect he will because of his interest in settling his case."

"So, I managed to find a hit on the Jim Reese obituary," Robbie says as he places the boiled corn on our plates, carefully buttering Katie's. "Get this, it turns out our demonic friend died two years ago."

"Two years?" Aileen is surprised by the news. "That means Jesse also died two years ago."

"Right? So, what does that tell you, Auntie?"

This is an interesting piece of information. Of course, although time does not concern the dead, it might be a shock for Jesse to realize he's been disconnected from the real world for so long.

"Thank you, Robbie, that's good information to go on, should Jim return. That means he's had two years to become the powerful entity he is." I look at the corn on the cob steaming on my plate and remove my reading glasses to wipe away the condensation.

"I want to go for a swim in the pool, Daddy," Katie blurts.

"After dinner, honey, you and I will swim." My nephew is a well-tempered father, unfazed by the little interruptions a child brings to every event. "Great auntie and Aileen have work to do upstairs. So, when they're doing that, we will swim. Promise."

This satisfies Katie, and she watches as Robbie cuts the corn from her cob, picking up the kernels with her tiny fingers and filing them into her mouth with buttery fingers. I watch, amused, as the evening sun attaches itself to her plump cheeks and feel my heart swell.

I understand I must protect my family from the Jim entity. His dark energy cannot be allowed to run rampant in my nephew's home. If that means forcing Jesse to cross over before he's ready, then that's what I will do. Nothing is more important than this little family. Nothing.

In the kitchen, we put away the dishes, then Robbie ushers Aileen and me out to finish our business upstairs. I kiss Katie on the top of her sun-kissed hair and follow Ai up to her room.

"There isn't any rhyme or reason for when Jesse shows up," Ai explains as we ascend the staircase. "We may be up here awhile."

"You just go about your usual routine, Ai. I will read my book while we wait," I reply, pulling the romance novel from my purse, carefully lowering myself into the plush couch.

And so we wait. By 8 PM, neither presence is felt. Perhaps Jesse has wandered too far this time. Perhaps Jim has caught up with him elsewhere. That would be disappointing. What we need now is Jesse's last name. If we can retrieve that, we can find his family and put any doubts they had about his death to rest. Once that is done, Jesse can move toward the light, and Jim should disappear.

Robbie gently knocks on the door to Ai's room at the base of the third-floor staircase and whispers loudly, "Would you both like a piece of cake?"

Ai nods at me, and I say, "Yes, please," in a louder tone than I expected. Robbie delivers two pieces of chocolate cake in his swimsuit.

"We haven't heard anything, so Katie thought you might be getting hungry up here. I'm going to read her to sleep in the family room so you can work up here if anyone shows up later."

"You're a saint, Robbie, thank you," I tell him, noticing Ai blush as she accepts her piece.

"This is just what I need to get through my last paper," Ai says from her desk, "A Sugar boost!" She forks a large piece of her cake into her grinning mouth.

"Okay," Robbie backs away and begins down the stairs. "May the force be with you," he says comically.

"And also with you," I reply, licking the icing off my fork.

Ten minutes later, Jesse arrives. *"Hi,"* he says, seemingly out of breath, but that can't be right. Can it? He's a ghost.

"Where have you been, Jesse?" Aileen is seated cross-legged on her bed, surrounded by schoolwork.

"I was recalling the night I was shot and transported to the scene. It felt surreal. I guess that's how I ended up here, though."

"You just visualize a place and arrive there?" I wonder. It's always interesting to know things from a ghost's perspective.

Jesse shrugs. I ask, "Jesse, what's your last name? We found Jim Reese's obituary, but we haven't looked for yours as we never got your last name."

"Oh, right, that's a necessary tool. Sorry, I don't know why I haven't offered it. My full name is Jesse Galligher. Jesse James Galligher."

"Your parents had a bit of fun with your name, I think, eh?" I write his full name in my sketchbook.

Jesse laughs, *"My father's idea. I think he wanted to will his son into being someone with a sense of adventure. Sadly, and disappointingly for him, he just got me."*

"Oh, I'm sure he's proud -" I begin, but am cut off.

"He's not, and now there will be no reason for him ever to be proud of me. I'm dead and have left nothing of worth for him to hold onto. He will remain disappointed in his only son. For that, I'm sorry, but I did try in the end. I really did."

"Oh, Jesse, I didn't mean to make you sad," I say, wishing I could hold him in a hug.

"I feel like I stole something from him, from both my parents, by dying like that. I stole the possibilities. Maybe I would have changed if given the chance to live. Maybe I'd have made them proud. But that's all over now. I have left this planet without making a mark." Jesse is wringing his hands again. *"I should have fought Jim off before he'd ever managed to corral me into that – but I-I did at the end. Too late, but I did. And I told him to fuck off."*

The last sentence catches me off guard, nearly choking on my last bite of cake. "You made progress, Jesse," I clear my throat. "That's important."

Ai is standing and approaching Jesse with a hand outstretched. "Jesse, don't do that. None of us knows how long we have."

He perks up a moment, hearing Ai's words. *"A little more time, and I would have finished my dissertation, at least. That would have meant something. It was a harsh method to uncover people's fears and unresolved issues, but it was mine."*

"Jesse, I'm going to give your name to my nephew now so he can find your family, and we can relay your story. We will also pass on Jim's confessions about murdering his wife and her lover. We will do all of that, and you can cross over."

"What's to cross over to for someone who only tormented others with his experiments?"

I don't know what lies ahead. I hope that no omnipotent being stands in judgment over us. But what do I say to soothe this poor boy's conscience? His guilt seems misplaced to me.

"Jesse, none of us can say for certain what happens next, but I don't believe in Heaven and Hell. I only believe in energy, and energy is eternal." I gesture to him as proof of that.

"You didn't carry out your experiments on others maliciously to satisfy some dark craving. I believe we know you well enough to understand that," I say, not entirely sure how well I actually know him. "You're a scientist. You were building a theory that would one day help others."

"That's true," Jesse admits reluctantly. *"I am a scientist in that I was merely gathering evidence to support my thesis."*

"So don't give it any more of your energy, dear. What comes next is what comes for us all. Please don't fear it. Embrace it." In all my years of practice, I've never given a ghost a pep talk.

Before I can begin coaching Jesse to find the light, he disappears. Aileen and I share a stunned glance.

"That was odd," Ai says, validating my feelings.

"But ... this is what he does," I remind her. "He thinks of a place and is transported. Maybe that's what just happened?"

Ai shrugs. "Do we wait for him to come back?"

"I'm going to get ready for bed," I say, stand, call down to Robbie, and he comes running.

Chapter 36 - Rob

After rushing to get my aunt's sketchbook, I went back to the kitchen island to look up Jesse James Galligher's obituary.

We now know he died two years earlier, along with Jim. So I searched the obituaries for Hamilton in 2023. But nothing appeared. Not even rearranging the names gave me anyone close to his age.

"What the ..." I'm stumped. "If they died on the same day and in the same city ... he's got to be listed." I redouble my efforts, extending my search. Perhaps he was taken to another city. Did he live in Hamilton, or was he merely a student here? They might have written his obituary in his hometown.

"That makes sense," I say to no one. Still, after an hour of searching obituaries, I am coming up empty.

"Maybe some people don't have funerals or write obits," I say aloud to the empty kitchen. It's late now, and I have to tear Katie away from the TV and get her ready for bed.

Once that is done, I say good night to Ai and my aunt. "No luck with the obituaries," I tell them.

"Widen your search, Robbie. He was a student here," my aunt suggests.

"I've done that. I don't understand it. There's no mention of him in any obituary anywhere."

"Okay, let's sleep on it. I'm exhausted," she says, grasping Ai's hand and letting go. They've become very close in such a short time. I'm happy for both. Having found each other like this. Two of a kind, I think.

"Works for me, goodnight," I say as I walk into Katie's room for one last kiss and then settle into my bed.

Chapter 37 - Sandi

Ai's footsteps thunder down the stairs, waking me with a knock on the basement wall of Robbie's guest room. I am startled awake, reaching for my glasses on the bedside table.

"I'm so sorry, Sandi," Ai begins, bent over my bed, a look of terror overtaking her pretty features. "He's back."

"Jesse?"

"No, Jim Reese," she says with a shudder. "He's very angry and is pushing furniture, tearing papers, and creating chaos."

I pull myself out of bed, noticing the fear in Aileen's voice. "Let's finish this once and for all," I say, mustering a confidence I don't usually possess at this hour.

"Thank you, thank you," Ai steps back as I straighten myself to my full five feet two inches in my gingham nightgown. A frightening sight, no doubt. Let's hope Jim Reese thinks so.

I follow Ai up the three flights, knees cracking all the way, passing Robbie and Katie's rooms as quietly as possible.

The air feels much cooler in Ai's attic room, where the furniture is askew and torn papers scatter across the original hardwood floors. Imagine if you could trap a ghost and use it as a kind of air conditioning. Clearly, I am not as awake as I should be.

"Enough is enough, Jim!" I whisper/scream, not generating the intensity I'd like to convey, but worried about waking Katie and Robbie.

"Bring me the boy!" Jim's disembodied voice commands. *"He is mine!"*

"What makes you say that? What claim do you have on the boy?" I stand in the centre of the room, my short hair whipping around the top of my head from the artificial breeze Jim has summoned.

"He's mine! He owes me a debt!"

"Seems tit for tat to me," I say pragmatically. "You shot him, he shot you. Who brought the gun with ill intent that night? *You* did that!" I explain as if he doesn't know. "You're the architect of your end, and we know your name. Jim Reese. You died two years ago. It is time for you to cross over."

"To where will I cross? I see no light beyond yours and the boys." His voice, though still inhuman, takes on a

melancholy tone we have not yet heard. *"I will take him with me wherever I go."*

"Where you go and where he goes may be two very different places," I warn. "You had murder in your heart that night. Jesse had only the will to survive you."

"Ha!" Jim scoffs, *"he has no will of his own. He barely gathered the courage to speak that night!"*

"But speak he did, and it was no small feat," I remind him. "Jesse did not speak in life as he does in death. He has confidence now that you cannot manipulate."

"I will take him," he assures me, *"I will drag him to Hell with me if that is where I am meant to go."*

Bats then suddenly materialize from the papers being whipped about in Jim's artificial windstorm. I duck and watch as Aileen does the same. The bats flutter about in tight circles, summoned by the darkness in Jim's soul. His abilities are frightfully impressive. He is manifesting visions that are particularly uncomfortable to me. I take issue with bats. I once had a bat trapped in my house that kept dive bombing Max and me. It took hours to get it out of the house.

Ai instinctively opens her window in hopes the bats will take their leave, and it pays off. The flying rats see their escape and burst through the open window.

Relieved, I then remember the others Jim had murdered and pause to summon their spirits, in case they still walked this realm. I call them forth as I speak their names. "Your wife, Carley Reese, and her lover, Lucas Guest, were also victims of yours."

"You know nothing of my wife," he spits.

"I know you murdered them as well. I know they are happy together. I know you are a wicked man."

"She betrayed me!" He's losing his grip, if ever he were a rational man to begin with.

"You did not *own* her, Jim!"

"She was my wife!"

"She was her own person!" I am now becoming animated. I have no patience for men who feel they own the women they've married.

"She had cheated on me before that. I forgave her."

"She didn't want your forgiveness, Jim," I say, as if I am processing information directly from Carley herself. "She wanted her freedom."

"She never asked for her freedom," he scoffs.

"What did you think cheating on you meant? She wasn't being cruel; she was being proactive. She wanted out and thought that was the only way you would let her go; if she betrayed your trust." I've lived long enough to know many couples whose marriages ended due to an affair. I've sat with both men and women who'd done the cheating, and their reasoning was all the same. They wanted their partner to leave them. They acted out rather than doing the respectful thing. I don't condone cheating, but I understand the root cause behind it. I decide to question Jim on his feelings toward his wife.

"Tell me, Jim, did you even love Carley?"

All activity in the room ceases. The breeze dies down. The furniture no longer scrapes along the hardwood. Even the temperature seems to regulate itself. I glance at Ai, and she stops rubbing her upper arms to keep warm.

"I loved her," Jim responds a moment later, in what I would call an unconvincing lie.

"No," I tell him. "You might have *needed* her, but you didn't *love* her. You can't commit to murdering someone you love."

"It was a crime of passion," he insists.

"No," I reiterate. "You waited for your moment. You plotted. You were in control of your actions. Passion is reserved for those who act out of emotional distress. You had time to consider your move. Just as you had time to consider murdering a young man whose only crime was in solving yours."

Jim is silent. The room's temperature fluctuates unpredictably. I sense emotional chaos filling the air. Maybe I am connecting with him.

"He did love me," a new voice enters the room, a soft, feminine voice.

"Who is this?" I ask, the hairs rising on my neck.

"Carley Reese," she says in a soothing tone. *"You did love me, Jim. I know that."*

"You're here," Jim's voice softens as I imagine it would have sounded in life when speaking to someone he admired. *"You came for me."*

"I came to help you; I came because she called," Carley's apparition appears before us. Jim also assumes his human shape, discarding the shadow form. Carley reaches for Jim's hands, and he offers them. Then Carley turns to address me. *"Thank you for your light,"* Carley says.

"I did love you," Jim reaffirms. Carley turns her attention back to him and nods.

"But you didn't respect me, Jim." Carley moves closer to her estranged husband. *"You kept me like a trophy. You kept me to yourself. You were suffocating me. I needed a way out. I took the only one I could live with."*

"I-I'm sorry if I was not the husband you deserved," Jim is becoming increasingly sedated as his dead wife speaks from the heart.

"I knew you were a man of fierce loyalty, Jim, a man who valued loyalty above all else. But you expected me to share your opinions, to serve only your needs. I had needs, too, Jim. So I used your inflated need for loyalty against us. Not just against you, my husband, but against both of us so that you would let me go."

"I didn't want to let you go, Carley. I didn't want to do this alone."

Emotion is getting the better part of him. *"You were my Skip."*

"But I wasn't, Jim. You wouldn't let me lead outside of the rink. I never had a voice with you beyond the game. I felt awful about the first affair. I made sure you found out. I wanted you to leave me. To hate me."

"I couldn't hate you. I didn't want to hate you, Carley."

"Yes, you forgave my infidelity to my chagrin. And I knew I couldn't convince you, Jim. You wouldn't have listened. Then Lucas entered our lives, and I fell in love again, Jim. Do you remember what that feels like? I felt seen. I felt cared for - not caged."

I exchange another glance with Ai and get the impression she, too, is growing uneasy with being caught in the middle of this marital exchange.

"I did a bad thing, Carley," he admits, head down, their hands still intertwined, a ghostly mist between them. *"I did a bad thing again. To keep my terrible secret."*

"I know I've contributed to your poor choices. I won't tell you otherwise. However, taking responsibility for your actions in response to my mistakes will give you clarity, Jim. It's the only way you can cross over."

Jim's head lifts to meet his wife's stare. *"Do you mean we could cross together?"*

"Yes, that's why I stayed behind. To right the wrongs I contributed to. In this moment, I still love you, Jim. Love doesn't die. Not here. Not where we're heading. I couldn't leave without sharing your burden. Leave this behind. Admit your wrongdoings and follow me."

A circular light manifests in the window behind Ai. It is all-encompassing. It is, I am certain, where all light originates. Pure. Overwhelmingly beautiful. It calls to me. It calls to us all in the end.

"I killed out of instinct," Jim confesses. *"I did it to protect myself. I did it out of ego, out of spite. I haven't lived a good life since, and I died a coward, taking another innocent life. I am not worthy of your love or your consideration."*

"And so now you may follow me into the light, Jim. You no longer have to exist in pain. With your confession comes forgiveness."

"But, Jesse, I need his forgiveness. I took his life to save my own."

"Jesse appreciates your heartfelt confession," she insists as she leads him past Aileen and toward the pulsating light. *"Jesse will be forever grateful for his interaction with you. You have changed him for the better, regardless of your intent. It's what souls do."*

"I don't understand," Jim's voice cracks and succumbs to his emotions.

"You will," she assures him as they disappear into the circle of light.

Ai drops to her knees, covering her face, overwhelmed by emotion. I stand in awe of what we've just seen, staring at the window where a faint imprint of the light still lingers in my vision.

Robbie joins us at the top of the staircase.

"You did it," he exclaims. "You vanquished Jim!"

"Carley did that," I insist, tearing my gaze away from the window. Aileen is quietly sobbing on her knees, hands still pressed into her face. Robbie moves to comfort her, as I had suspected he would. It is his nature to console others.

Chapter 38 - Aileen

"Thank you, Rob," I say, feeling embarrassed to be so emotional, but the tragedy and compassion that just unfolded here were compelling. I stand partly on my own and partly supported by Rob's firm grip.

"What time is it?"

"Uh," Rob looks at his wrist, but there is no watch to be found. "Shit, I, uh,"

"It's 3:30 in the morning," Sandi offers. "It's been another long night." My bed squeaks as Sandi sits heavily on it.

"A half past the Witching hour," Rob says ironically. Sandi nods. I had not heard of this before.

"I don't know this hour," I say, looking for clarity.

"It's Western folklore," Sandi begins, "but folklore is often borne of truth. The Witching hour, or Devil's hour, is proposed to be the opposite of when Christ died on the cross. The Bible puts his death at 3 PM, and so 3 AM becomes the Devil's hour. I don't buy into the Christian canon like that, but I support that paranormal activity is heightened between the hours of midnight and 3 AM from a lifetime of experiences."

"Ah," I say, connecting this to a Japanese myth. "Then it is like the Ushi no toki mairi." I watch Rob's eyes grow wider at the mention. His interest spikes.

"This is when a curse is most effective. Between 1 AM and 3 AM, the hour of the Ox," I tell them. "When the Kibune deity is believed to have visited the shrine where the curse must be enacted.

"The curse came later, though," I say, recalling the myth more completely. "At first it was just a time to wish for things when the Deity was present."

"So many similarities across so many cultures," Sandi says as if caught up in a trance of her own. She shakes her head. "The world never ceases to amaze me."

"Seriously," Robbie agrees. "How can two cultures separated by such vast distances and histories share a common, and completely random, detail like the time of day spirits are most active?"

"Because it is true," I say, and both Sandi and Robbie laugh inwardly at this. It amuses me that I can make others laugh.

"Why has Jesse not returned?" I turn to Sandi for the answer.

"He seems to be on a different schedule," Sandi replies. "He said he jumps around from place to place almost unconsciously."

Then, as if summoned merely by speaking his name, Jesse materializes in front of us.

"Ears burning?" Sandi asks him with a snicker. Rob turns to look at who his aunt is speaking to. Of course, he can not see Jesse's tall, looming form as we can.

"He's back?" He asks me, and I nod.

Sandi stands and covers her mouth as if experiencing a revelation.

Chapter 39 - Sandi

I feel faint yet invigorated simultaneously. Something occurs to me as I lay eyes on Jesse this time, tracing the recent events to a new conclusion. This discovery raises the hairs on the back of my neck and sends a satisfying thrill from the top of my head to the tips of my toes.

"Listen," I begin, shaking my finger in Jesse's direction, desperate to reveal the information that has been granted me. "When I was rhyming off types of ghosts the other night, I failed to mention one that, though extremely rare, may better fit Jesse's description than any other," I admit, having weighed the evidence in this moment.

"I believe Jesse is what's referred to as a *Living* ghost."

"Sounds like an oxymoron," Robbie says dismissively.

"Doesn't it?" I refocus. "Sometimes, and this would be my first experience with it, the living can project their spirit or ghost-self to another location to either save them from the suffering their physical body is experiencing or to warn a loved one of impending doom. Jesse told you to change Katie's carpet because he feared she would develop asthma. Jesse," I point to him, "how did you come by this information?"

"I-I don't know. When Ai asked me to visit Rob on the floor below that night, I heard Katie crying, and I felt compelled to get him out of bed."

"You pushed him and froze him out, he told me," I recount. "And we're grateful you did. You did nothing wrong. Then, you told Ai to relay to Robbie that Katie may develop asthma if they don't pull up the old rug."

"Yes, it just popped into my mind as I followed Rob into Katie's room. I don't know how it happened. It just did."

"You accessed the *ether*," I tell him. "Because you're in a deep state of meditation. You're not dead at all, Jesse, you're likely in a ... *coma*."

"A coma? You mean ... I'm alive!?"

"It's why we can't find you in any obituaries." My goodness, it's all starting to make sense. A shiver runs through my old bones. "It's also why you come and go. Your unconscious state is calling your spirit back to the last place you remember. Where you believe you'd died." I want to grab Jesse by the arms and pull him in for a hug.

"Jesse," I laugh aloud, "you're alive!" And then he vanishes.

Chapter 40 - Aileen

Jesse vanishing again upon Sandi's announcement is startling, but I realize I have information to support her claim of a Living Ghost, and I'm busting to tell her.

"Ikiryō!" I announce, my breath catching in my throat as I speak the name. I inhale sharply, surprised to find another similarity to Sandi's Western mythology. "It is more folklore from Japan. It means a person who can leave their body and haunt people and places while alive."

Sandi, placing her hands on her lap, the smile still on her face from her own eureka moment, says, "Please, tell us."

"Ikiryō is known by many names: Shōryō, Seirei, Ikisudama. It's used both literally and figuratively. What I mean is Ikiryō can also refer to a person who is disconnected from the world—someone who feels ignored or insignificant in life," I continue.

"Jesse told us he felt that way," Sandi offers, shaking her head. "Remember, he told us that he didn't feel connected to the world. That he was only here as an observer."

"Sounds like social anxiety," Robbie suggests. "Not participating in life."

"Exactly," Sandi agrees, acknowledging Rob and turning back to me.

"It is an out-of-body experience," I add, needing to verbalize my thoughts before they vanish. "Some believe that if a grudge or desire for vindication over a wrongful act requires action, a person can take on the Ikiryō form to right those wrongs. I studied this when I was younger, back when I thought I saw the ghost of a friend who was very much alive. She was spending the night with me, sleeping in my bed. I went to the bathroom, where I found her transparent form standing next to me. It was frightening because I thought she had died and become a ghost. I rushed back to my room and found her there asleep. I checked her breathing and turned to see her spirit moving into my room. I shook her awake. Once she awoke, her ghost disappeared."

"Wow. Did she remember being out of body?" Rob asks, riveted by my story.

"Yes, and she told me years later, when we reconnected and I reminded her of the event, that she'd never experienced it again."

"Fascinating," Sandi says, hanging on my words, and just like when I first told Rob about the ghost in his home, I feel seen.

"There are many stories about Ikiryō in my country. They can appear in various forms, not only in their original human shape but also as a severed head, a fireball, or even as a curse.

"Also, an Ikiryō, it's been said, can sometimes possess a person to accomplish their task. But that is rare."

"Your culture seems to be the authority on curses," Rob says comically. I only smirk at his comment, too engrossed in the bizarre conclusion we've arrived at by connecting two distinct cultural myths in explaining Jesse's diagnosis.

"I think we've found an explanation for Jesse's condition," Sandi insists. "If he reappears, we can give him more information. If not, perhaps he's waking up from his coma?"

Chapter 41 - Rob

"That's ... ahhh," I say, feeling upset with myself for not checking hospitals too. "But wait, come on, Auntie, he's a ghost! You guys *saw* him; he's a *ghost*." My arms flail as I turn in a circle, using the dishevelled room as proof.

"A *living* ghost," my aunt reprimands me, "Or Ikiryō, as Ai put it." She stands abruptly, "Robbie, check the hospitals."

I pull out my iPad and type Jesse James Galligher into the search engine. I find half a dozen news articles mentioning him. My hands go to the top of my head as I exhale in exasperation. A chuckle escapes me.

"Yup, there he is. Is this him?" I turn my screen to the women, and they nod. I was too specific in my search terms before, looking only for a dead man.

"Unbelievable!" I utter, skimming an article. "Says here he was found bleeding out on the paved path in Bayfront Park right here in Hamilton, and was miraculously revived. So, he *did* die." I scan further down the article. "But they brought him back. The problem was he'd lost so much blood that he slipped into a coma."

"And that's how you get a living ghost," Sandi exclaims, clapping her hands together. The sharp slap of her palms makes me jump.

"Is it Hamilton General he is at?" Ai asks, having visited there with her nursing class to observe the ER.

"Uh," I read a little further, "yes, Ham Gen."

"I'm sorry," Ai says, yawning, "this is all very incredible, but I need to sleep. Can we discuss this again tomorrow night?"

"Yes, sorry, Ai, we'll let you get some sleep. I need to sleep too. I have six clients tomorrow. I don't know why I do that to myself," I say, knowing full well it's because I can't say no to a client in need.

"Thank you so much, Sandi," Ai says as she embraces my aunt. "You're a real miracle."

I help my aunt down the steep stairs to the second level, then to the main floor. She turns on the kettle.

"Don't you want to get some sleep, Auntie?" I'm ready to drop.

"Won't be much use, Robbie," she tells me, rolling her head over her neck, popping the joints. It's a satisfying sound. I hear it a lot on the massage table. "I'll drink my camomile and see how that goes."

"Okay, I'm going to check on Katie and then crawl back into bed," I say, giving her frail back a quick rub over the satin finish of her gingham nighty. "Great work tonight."

My aunt offers a tired smile and nods, closing her eyes as she leans against the kitchen island. "It was quite a success, dear. I'm very glad Carley came back for Jim. That's one ghost off our plate."

I return to bed, and although tempted to continue researching Jesse's case, including finding his parents, I simply cannot resist the exhaustion and fall into a deep sleep.

Chapter 42 - Jesse

I'm *alive.* I can hardly believe what Sandi's telling me. I'm alive? I'm in a coma?! That I'm projecting myself onto these people in an unconscious attempt to solve my mystery. It's mind-boggling. I'm gobsmacked. I'm ... *alive!*

As if at the realization, I'm torn away from Ai's bedroom, suddenly stumbling upon my material self as if my spirit knows where my body is. I'm floating above myself. I'm in a hospital bed. I have a mustache. Someone's been messing around with my facial hair.

There are tubes in my nose and mouth, and I suspect they are coming from other parts of my body. I look peaceful. My hair is messy and much longer than I've ever kept it. I like it. It covers my high forehead.

Upon further inspection, I find there are tubes in my arm. Some patches on my chest are connected to another machine. Blinking lights and beeping sounds accompany a screen that shows my heartbeat. It seems stable, if television dramas are any indication of the real thing.

I look around the room and see two other beds with unresponsive residents. Are they also in comas? How long can someone remain in this state? Sandi told me Jim has been gone for two years now. That means I've been in a coma for two years. I recall hearing that some people wake up after decades in a coma. That's a comforting thought.

This isn't a great outcome, though. I'm alive, but— am I really alive in this state? Am I a vegetable? If I wake up, will I have brain damage? If I wake up, will I be able to work on myself? To become a real person and not the dud I was before my murder. Correction - attempted murder.

The door to my shared room opens, and an older woman with a stethoscope around her neck guides a group of twenty-somethings in white lab coats inside. They pass by my roommates and circle around my unflinching body.

What if I never wake up? Does that mean I'll be like this until someone unplugs me? Then what? Do I get sucked into the light? I guess this is why I haven't seen the light. I'm not dead. A living ghost, Sandi called me.

I watch and listen as the student body pokes and prods my husk. One is asked to insert a needle into my forearm as if I were *Cavity Sam* in the Children's *Operation* game. I half expect to see my nose light up red, but there are no panicked sounds to alarm the 'doctors' when the young man sinks the needle into my flesh.

I desperately want to re-enter my body, sit up, and slap this kid. That would shock the hell out of them, wouldn't it! How satisfying that would be. But for all my wanting, I can't seem to force this outcome.

What about my parents? I should see them. Try to connect with them as I have with Sandi and Aileen. I visualize my childhood home and find myself there in less time than it once took to blink. It seems ghosts have mastered teleportation quite handily.

I walk through the modest home, moving from room to room. I stop in my bedroom, which hasn't changed since I left it after the Christmas holidays. Nothing on the walls—no posters or pictures of me with friends. I've truly robbed myself of a life by not speaking and hiding behind excuses.

I had no favourite bands, no comics, and hardly any books beyond a few psychology tomes. My sheets weren't decorated with logos of sports teams. Ah, but there is my Rubik's Cube. I spent hours with it. I would have asked my parents to take me to a tournament if winning against my peers held any interest for me. But then, what peers?

This room stands as a sad reminder of a life not fully lived. And why? Because I couldn't summon the interest, courage, or whatever was holding me back just to join in a conversation, let alone start one.

I see myself through my father's eyes. He wasn't angry with me all those years; he was sad for me, and that sadness turned into frustration, then anger, then disinterest, and eventually the nothingness we shared.

Allowing myself a moment to see my life through my mother's eyes is even more painful. She was my cheerleader, always hoping for the best. I know I broke that hope more than once, but she continued to believe in me.

I admit I was disconnected from reality. Not entirely my fault, though I understand now that much of my mutism was a choice rather than a reflex. Not engaging became part of who I am. I don't want to be that person anymore, and if given the chance, I vow not to be.

I enter my parents' room, where they sleep back-to-back. They look peaceful. I wonder about their health. My coma must be taking a toll on them. They seem older than their fifty-odd years. How old are they now? Fifty-seven and fifty-nine, I think.

How can I possibly communicate all this regret to my parents now? I'm unresponsive, lying in the hospital for up to two years. They've probably lost hope that I will ever wake up. Why haven't they pulled the plug?

Hope. That's why, and my mother was brimming with it.

Chapter 43 - Rob

After work, I mow the lawn and weed the gardens, waiting for my aunt to arrive with Katie. Ai arrives first and greets me in my postage-stamp-sized front yard.

"Hey, Ai, how was your day? School or work today?" I can never keep the days straight.

"Work today," Aileen is a PSW at a retirement home downtown. "That nasty old man actually hit me today," she exclaims, wide-eyed, revealing her disbelief.

"What?!" I rub the dirt off my hands with my pants.

"Yes, the one I've told you about, who is always looking at me angrily? *Him*. He hates Asians, I think." She nods, closing her eyes hard. I stifle a smile as I find her quirky nods endearing.

"The one with dementia? I've heard it can bring out the worst in some." I'm not defending the old man; he could just be a racist asshole, but I don't want to make Ai feel any worse about it.

"Yes, maybe, but his diaper's not going to change itself," she cackles at her remark. I've never heard a belly laugh from Ai, but this will do. "Is Sandi coming tonight?"

"Yeah, and we'll find out where Jesse's parents are and try to contact them." I return to the front garden as Ai walks up the steps to the porch. "Oh, and did you have any visits last night or today from Jesse?"

"No, nothing," she says, leaning over the railing, "I hope to tonight." She disappears into the house.

It's Friday, and I'm looking forward to sleeping in tomorrow, so I hope any activity that comes up tonight is over quickly.

As I prepare dinner for all of us, Aunt Sandi enters through the front door with Katie, who is chatting away about a boy named Jeremy from her preschool.

"Is he real or is he a spirit?" I hear my aunt ask.

"Well, I pinched him, and he said ow," Katie responds mischievously.

"Oh! Then, human," Auntie replies resolutely. "But be careful, pinching isn't very nice."

"I got in trouble," Katie explains. "It's okay though, Auntie, I don't get in trouble much." Her high ponytail sways as she shakes her head.

"Hello," I say, as I lift my daughter and thank my aunt for bringing her over. "How about spaghetti for dinner? It's almost ready."

"My favourite!" Katie squeals. I put her down, and she runs to the island where her colouring books await.

My aunt places her overnight bag on the front bench. "After dinner, we solve this mystery?"

I nod, "Yes, please!" As invigorating as a ghost in my house has been, it's also been draining – on all of us.

After dinner, I do the dishes so Aileen and my aunt can discuss next steps at the dining table. They are within earshot, so I am not left out.

"When Robbie finds Jesse's parents on the internet, we'll plan to meet them at the hospital," Auntie explains. "I feel we should visit Jesse in person."

"That will be so weird," Ai admits, drawing out the 'e' in weird with a smile inching up the right side of her face.

"Yes, I don't disagree with you, Ai," Auntie submits, "but I'd like to get my hands on Jesse. I want to get a sense of his well-being."

"Can you do that?" I ask, turning to face them as I dry a pot.

"I might get a feeling, yes. Something that could indicate how far removed from our world his spirit actually is."

"And what about his parents? What can we offer them?" I've moved on to pouring myself a glass of wine. Ai doesn't drink, but my aunt shows two fingers, which I pour into her glass.

"I'd like to be able to tell them whether he will emerge from his coma and in what condition. You know, dear, comas are often a death sentence."

"And after two years -" I say, cutting myself off. I mean, that's a long time.

"It would be a shame if he were never to return to the world of the living," Auntie states. "He is an intelligent boy with much to offer the world."

"You said before you have allowed a ghost to possess you." Ai's statement raises my aunt's eyebrows. We both know what she's digging at. "What is that called again ... being a medium?"

"As I've told you both, I have channelled before," she replies, a hint of unease in her voice. "But remember, Ai, Jesse is not a ghost or spirit. Not really."

"No, he is Ikiryō," Ai reiterates her previous point, "and it is said they, too, can possess a person to accomplish their task."

"Fascinating, Ai," my aunt says, genuinely surprised by the statement. "So Jesse would simply have to accept my invitation?"

"I believe that if they want it enough, they do not need an invitation." Ai leans back in her chair.

"Oh, my, dear, he would *need* an invitation to enter *my* body," her tone is again resolute, but she winks, and Ai cackles for the second time today. "But a very interesting concept. If I could channel Jesse and let him speak for himself through me, he could have a conversation with his parents."

"That. Is. Freaky," I say honestly, draining my glass. "I will have to come to this. Just seeing him in the flesh will be awesome."

Later in the evening, as Katie watches one of her many children's shows in the living room, my Auntie, Aileen, and I remain at the dining table. We're seated three across, so we can all see my screen as I search for Jesse James Galligher's parents.

The search doesn't take long. Jesses' father is a businessman in good standing with the Toronto Chamber of Commerce. Through that site, I retrieved his email and used it to reverse search his phone number. I also obtained a physical address.

"So, who wants to make the call?" I ask, glancing at my wristwatch. It's 7:15 PM.

"I'll do the talking, Robbie," Auntie tells us. Ai is relieved, and, honestly, so am I. I pull out my cell phone, place it on the table, turn on the speaker function, and dial the number.

After two rings, a woman answers, "Hello?"

My aunt answers, "Yes, hello, is this Mrs. Galligher? June Galligher?"

"It is," the voice on the other end sounds withdrawn, as if expecting bad news.

"My name is Sandi Burmeister, a medium for those who have passed," she says, making a face as if she had screwed up. She pushes the mute button and whispers, "Oh, dear, now she's going to think her son is dead."

"A what?" Mrs. Galligher sounds taken aback. Auntie presses the mute button again to speak.

"Oh, uh, a medium, Mrs. Galligher. I've been in contact with your son, Jesse; he's visited me from his coma." Auntie looks at me and then at Ai, and shrugs.

"I'm sorry, what? My son? Yes, he's in a coma. Is this ... are you a reporter?" She is not listening.

"No. Ma'am. I'm a medium -"

"Medium what?" I press the mute button before I burst out laughing. I know, I know, it's awful, but stress affects people differently. "Hello?" I unmute.

"I speak to the dead, Mrs. Galligher."

"My son is not dead. He's in a coma."

"Yes, but he has travelled outside his body and come to me in spirit form to tell me his story. I want to share it with you."

"What is this? This isn't real." She's becoming defensive, but given how we're approaching this, it's understandable she questions the validity of our call. I feel like a kid making crank calls.

"I'm sorry, Mrs. Galligher. May I call you June? I don't mean to upset you; I am simply trying to share information your son conveyed to me."

"Why now? He's been in a coma for twenty-odd months. What could he have told you?"

"It's not old news, June; it's new information about the attempt on his life."

"That Jim Reese got his," she says. "My boy never owned any guns. He shot my boy and got shot himself. It was self-defence, the Police said."

"Exactly, June, and that's what Jesse told me just three nights ago. What I'm offering is a chance for you to speak with your son." Auntie's gaze falls on me.

"*Speak* with Jesse? How?" Was that hope in her voice?

"I would channel Jesse, and he could speak through me."

Silence. Deafening silence. I feel the energy in the room become charged. Even Katie's gaze breaks with the TV as she looks over from her beanbag chair.

"Why are you doing this?" June sounds hoarse. "This is cruel."

"Oh, June, no, please, you can look me up. I really am a medium, and Jesse *has* contacted me."

"Are you saying he's dead? My son is dead?"

"No, June, he's very much alive, but he's travelled outside of himself and contacted me. I want to give you the opportunity to speak with him. I want to meet you at the hospital and channel your son."

"Why would you want to do that?"

"I want to give you that gift, June."

"Prove it," June says, adopting a no-nonsense tone. We three glance at one another.

"I-I'm going to tell you something he told me about the night he – the night he first met Jim Reese," my aunt wipes her brow.

Silence. June is waiting.

"I only know this because it's part of the bigger picture of why Jim did what he did. You see, Jesse was researching a cold case involving Jim Reese. It goes back a couple of decades. It has to do with Jim's wife and -"

"And a curling medalist," June finishes the sentence. "Lucas something. How could you know this?"

"Because Jesse told me," My aunt breathes a sigh of relief. We all do.

"Only the police investigators knew what Jesse was researching on his laptop," she pauses. "They took everything from his rented basement, and that's what they found."

"Okay, good, then you have proof. I'm not affiliated with the Hamilton Police Service. I wouldn't have known what was on Jesse's laptop." My Auntie offers us a thumbs up.

"No, I don't suppose you would." Silence as I imagine June rolling this over in her head and heart. "It was never disclosed why Jim Reese shot my son, because there was no evidence to support that he had anything to do with his wife's disappearance."

"Jesse provided us with more details about the Reese cold case. Jim had confessed to his wife's murder. We can share this information with the police to help bring you some peace regarding why this terrible thing happened to Jesse." My aunt shares a satisfied look with both Ai and me. She's making headway.

"And you say I could *talk* to him? To my son?" Her voice trembles.

"I will do everything in my power to make that happen, June. Can we meet at the hospital tomorrow?"

Silence.

"Yes. We can." She trails off. "Wait, what will this cost?"

"It's a gift, June," Auntie explains. "I want nothing but to let Jesse tell you what he's told us. To reconnect with your son."

"That's very kind," June tells us.

Once the times are scheduled and Jesse's room number given, I hang up the phone.

"That was not easy," I say. Ai shakes her head in agreement.

"That was a first," my aunt tells us, resting her forehead on the dining table. "I'm too old for this," she says, and we all share a tired chuckle.

"Now we just need Jesse to come back so we can tell him the plan," Ai says with her trademark nod.

My aunt gets up from the table. "I'm going home," she says. I need to be in top form tomorrow evening if this is going to work." She turns to Aileen. "If Jesse returns, please explain our plan. I think he should be very happy to do this with his parents."

"I will," Ai places a supportive hand on my aunt's arm and stands to see her out.

I stand too and walk my aunt to her car. "This might be your best ghost story yet, Auntie," I tell her.

"That, my dear, remains to be seen."

Chapter 44 - Sandi

The following afternoon, at Hamilton General, Robbie, Aileen, and I follow the green stripe on the laminate flooring to Jesse's floor and room number. Katie has been left with her mother.

I hesitate at the open door, my pulse pounding. I take a deep, calming breath to steady my nerves and squeeze both Ai and Robbie's hands, who are standing on either side of me.

"I've done house calls before," I tell them, "But nothing quite like this."

Ai had not been visited by Jesse last night or today. And I'm concerned I may not be able to reach him now. It will be a devastating blow to his parents if I can't. Another deep breath, and I release their grips and charge forward.

Inside the room, we pass two other beds before reaching Jesse's. He has a window with a view of a brick wall and is separated from the other two patients by a heavy curtain. No need to pander to views in the coma ward, I suppose.

Now exposed to Jesse's physical form, I am taken aback. I inhale and hold my breath with a hand to my chest. He's thinner than his apparition. Of course, he would be. He's pale, too. His hair longer. Curls wrapping around his gaunt cheekbones. I remember to exhale and turn my attention to the middle-aged couple seated at his bedside. They turn to acknowledge us, and I replace my expression with a sympathetic smile.

"Hello," I manage, "I'm Sandi," I gesture to Robbie and Aileen, "This is my nephew Robbie, who's home Jesse appeared in, and this is Aileen, who made first contact with your son."

The couple stands hesitantly and extends their hands for a shake. We take turns, and June signals for us to sit. They've found two more chairs and a stool to fit us all.

"This isn't some kind of hoax, right?" June's husband, Jesse's father, asks immediately, then clears his throat.

"My credentials are all online, as I told your wife over the phone, Todd, may I call you Todd?" He shakes his head, yes. I'm beginning to feel more at ease.

"I don't understand how our son's *ghost* visited you all when he's clearly not passed," Todd starts defensively. "I don't even believe in ghosts."

"You don't have to believe in ghosts for them to exist," I assure them. "And it's true, Jesse has not passed, but there is another explanation for what we've been experiencing with your son."

"He is Ikiryō," Ai breaks in, "a living ghost. This is a very real occurrence in Japanese culture."

They stare blankly at her. "But he's not Japanese," June insists vacantly.

"A living ghost is very much a Western phenomenon as well," I interject. "Jesse's spirit or astral body, or consciousness if you like, has moved beyond the physical realm to seek help in solving the attempt on his life as well as closing the cold case against Jim Reese's other victims."

They nod in unison; June's fingers are intertwined with her son's. "You said you could channel Jesse. Do you mean his consciousness then?"

I nod, "Yes. He has been very active over the past few nights, but we didn't hear from him last night, so I don't want to disappoint you if he doesn't come through today. I will do everything I can to summon him, but it's up to him to accept the invitation."

Jesse's parents look at each other and nod. "I think we understand ... as best we can," June says apologetically. "We're not spiritual people. We don't hold much stock in any of that." She looks at Todd, and he confirms her statement with another nod.

"It's healthy to be skeptical," I tell them, "But I'm not asking for compensation for doing this. Please take solace in that, and know I am only here for you both, and for Jesse." I want to reach out with a reassuring hand but stifle the urge.

June smiles weakly and asks, "Do you need to touch him, or -"

"Yes, with your permission, that would be very helpful." I accept her nod as approval and take Jesse's hand, offered by his mother. It is warm after her firm grip on it. "Robbie, please, get the door."

I close my eyes and set my intention on Jesse's aura as he'd presented it to me in the past.

Chapter 45 - Jesse

I'm not sure why I keep revisiting the place where I was shot. It's compelling, I suppose. Certainly, it marks a significant milestone in my life, such as it was. No one could argue that. I think about the blood loss and what my blood might have mixed with as it flowed out of my body. Has it helped the soil at the edge of the sidewalk grow a particular type of plant? Did ants build a colony nearby and feed on my diminishing supply?

Strange, unwanted thoughts. Then I blink away from my crime scene and arrive at my professor's class, which is in session. A rare Saturday afternoon elective. Maybe seven kids in attendance.

Professor Sanders is giving one of his lively lectures about the psychology of social behaviour. This is perhaps the class that inspired my thesis on uncomfortable silences. These are first-year students. An exciting time in their post-secondary education. This is where their curiosities will develop into lifelong interests and potentially lead to careers.

I remember the feeling. It was akin to the butterflies I felt with each experiment unfolding at a party or event. It seems a waste to have lost all that research.

Suddenly, I feel a pull on my consciousness. Something is drawing me away from this moment to join another. I want to stay and watch the professor, absorbing his knowledge, but the pull grows stronger, and I feel compelled to follow.

Blink, and I find myself in my hospital room, floating above my body. There are others here. I shift my spirit form to align with these people. My parents are visiting, and Sandi, Ai, and Rob have joined them. The pull I feel toward Sandi is now all-encompassing. What is she doing? What does she want?

"I am inviting you to speak through me," Sandi repeats. Does she mean me? Is she asking what I think she's asking?

"Jesse James Galligher, use me as your conduit to share your story. Your parents are eagerly waiting to hear from you."

I feel goosebumps rise on my skin, if that's possible for a spirit. Then I examine my physical body's exposed forearm and see the tiny bumps appear. So I *am* connected to this body. That's reassuring.

Sandi has made her intention clear to me. I sense that. She's inviting me to use her as my voice. How do I manage that, though? Maybe I should also set an intention to accept Sandi's invitation.

Upon telling myself 'I accept', I am drawn into Sandi's living, breathing form. She takes a halting breath, and I feel it enter her lungs. This sensation is both exciting and distressing. I focus on her breath and imagine exhaling. Then inhaling. And repeat. I open Sandi's eyes and see the world as it is once more through the human experience. The veil of death, or near-death, is lifted. People are more than mere auras. My surroundings are in vivid colour again. I hear the world as it is. I have regained my five senses but lost the sixth.

"H-Hello?" I try out Sandi's mouth. I make an audible sound. I don't sound like myself, but I'm making progress.

"Jesse?" Mom asks pensively.

"Y-Yes," I say. "Is this real?"

Mom has a hand over her mouth, silencing a sound. Dad is gripping the armrests of his chair, his knuckles turning white.

Sandi interrupts my newfound power for a moment to say, "I've reached Jesse, please, ask any questions you need to."

"Jesse? Are you okay?" Mom is trembling, and Dad lifts his hand from the armrest to hold hers.

"I'm okay, Mom. I can't believe this is possible. I'm okay."

Mom breaks down, and Dad seizes the chance to gather proof that I am who I claim to be. Always the pessimist.

"Tell me something only you and I would know, son," he's leaning forward, still with mom's hand in his.

I reflect on my history and land on one thing I know I never told Sandi or Aileen. "The first words I uttered when I was four," I tell him, "I told you both that the man in our living room was a 'precocious flirt pandering to your perceived fears.'" The man in question was a literal vacuum salesman.

Dad is thrown back into his chair as if pushed by the weight of my words. "My god," he utters, his free hand covering his mouth. Mom looks up and studies my eyes – Sandi's eyes.

"Your eyes," she says to Sandi – me, "were they always green?"

Robbie shifts in his seat to look his aunt in the eye and confirms they were never green. "What the ... no, my aunt's eyes are blue."

"She has acquired that aspect of the Ikiryō, uh, of Jesse," Aileen announces, also craning her neck to see.

"This is unbelievable," Mom squeaks out. "Jesse, tell us what you need to tell us, honey. We're listening." She places her phone on my stomach to record me.

I start by saying, "I'm so sorry I did this. You don't deserve this."

"Son," my father says, "your thesis. It's brilliant. I want to tell you — I've always wanted to tell you how proud I am." His pride blends with regret, and he breaks down. I feel the tight knot forming in Sandi's throat over what he's just told me, but I swallow it down.

"I'm sorry I couldn't communicate properly in life," I say, needing to start by apologizing for who I was. "It was never you. It was always me."

"Oh, Jesse," Mom reaches out with her other hand to take Sandi's - mine. It feels good. It feels incredible to connect with my mom again like this. In this moment, I can appreciate why, once a spirit or demon possesses a person, they fight so hard to maintain that earthly connection. I've missed this.

After a deep, purifying breath, I describe the cold case; Jim's malicious intent, and the location of his wife's and the gold medalist's rings. I tell them where to find the bodies and how my investigation led me to Jim, as I continued piecing together his role in the disappearances. I explained this is why Jim approached me. This is why he shot me. To silence me.

"Tell the Police to visit the curling rink. They'll find the rings under the middle sheet below the Center circle."

"This is incredible, Jesse," Dad says, his throat raw. He is holding Sandi's other hand.

"Can you come back to us, Jesse?" Mom sounds hopeful. But then, she always has.

"I-I don't know, Mom," I stammer. I wish it were as easy as entering Sandi, but my still body has no power to summon or invite me in.

"Do any of you know how he could accomplish that?" Dad asks pleadingly to Rob and Aileen.

"The Ikiryō may reanimate once their task is complete," Ai tells them. This is encouraging news. So, how do I accomplish it?

"How do I do this, Ai?" I speak directly to the woman I first approached in my ghostly form. It's so bizarre to see her as she is and not merely light. She is beautiful in both incarnations.

"Are you satisfied that you have corrected the wrongs necessary to find peace?"

"I am. I have nothing more to tell," I justify. "The only other wrong I wished to right is to tell my parents how sorry I am that I treated them so unfairly."

"Oh, Jesse, listen to you now," Mom says, tightening her grip on Sandi's hand. "You're talking up a storm!" She chuckles despite herself. "You've learned so much."

"Can you forgive me?"

Tears stream down both my parents' reddening faces. "Of course," they say in unison. "Come back to us, Jesse," my father says in his commanding tone.

"Set your intention, Jesse," Sandi tells me. "Set your intention to return to your body. It could be as easy as teleporting from one place to another for you."

Suggesting the teleportation method is useful. Why couldn't I just teleport back into myself?

I consider the facts. "What if I never wake up?" It's a real possibility. I have no control over when or if I wake up.

"You will," Ai tells me, and I've never heard such conviction from her.

"I want to, of course, but I'm scared. What if I end up in a vegetative state?"

"Oh, honey, you're not a vegetable," Mom says, a hint of a laugh flickering at the edge of her voice. "It's true you lost over 40 percent of your blood volume that night, which then stopped your heart. The paramedics got it going again, but you went into hypovolemic shock, which drove you into a coma. Your blood pressure had dropped so low ... it was a miracle you survived."

"The doctors have told us that your brain did not suffer too prolonged a period of oxygen deprivation," Dad says. "And your mother and I have been reading by your bedside three or four times a week. If anyone should come out of a coma, it's you, son."

Chapter 46 - Sandi

I feel Jesse leave my body as if I've been shaken awake. Allowing him access to my senses was different from when I've channelled an actual spirit—someone who'd passed on. Still, it was very successful.

My eyes settle on Jesse's resting body. I loosen his parents' grips on my hands and curl my fingers into a fist, cracking the joints. "How long?" I ask.

"Uh, about fifteen minutes, Auntie," Robbie says. "Are you okay?"

"Yes, thank you," I straighten my back, roll my neck, and look at June and Todd as they wait for any further information from me.

"That was incredible, Sandi," June says, her eyes redder than I remember before going under Jesse's spell.

"I'm so glad Jesse came through for you. He's going to attempt to re-enter his body," I look back at Jesse, watch the machines move his chest up and down, and wait for a sign he has returned.

"I-I could get a doctor in here," Todd announces, "there is a drug they can give that might speed things up ... like a dopamine accelerator, amantadine."

I suggest that a doctor might be a good idea, if only to help Jesse when he wakes up.

Todd leaves to fetch a doctor. June looks hopeful. We're all going through this for the first time. I glance at Robbie, and he smiles brightly at me—as supportive as ever. Aileen is now covering her mouth, staring at Jesse.

All eyes are on Jesse. Will he, won't he? I feel the pressure building behind my eyes. This was my idea: to come here and offer this service to these good people. If Jesse doesn't wake up, I'm afraid ... well, I'm afraid. For his parents. What will this do to them? Is it enough that they had the chance to talk to their son?

"Did his finger just move?" Ai is nodding at Jesse, both hands still covering her mouth. I lean in.

"Holy shit," Robbie says, startling everyone. "His finger!"

June springs from her chair to see. "Uh, it *is* moving!" she says excitedly.

Todd rushes in, followed by the doctor behind him. "What's happening?"

"Jesse's finger is moving," June points out. "Doctor, can you wake him up?"

"Please, everyone, clear the bed," the doctor orders, examining the finger in question. "Sometimes the nerves will involuntarily give the impression that the patient is moving on their own."

I know it's Jesse in there.

Next, his entire hand twitches, causing the doctor to step back. "O ... K," he says, uncertain of what is happening. He pulls a penlight from his coat pocket and lifts Jesse's eyelids to check his pupils.

"We have dilation," he tells us. Then Jesse's eyelids squeeze tightly and open slowly. "Jesse, can you hear me?"

Jesse nods. June and Todd hug as Robbie, Aileen, and I share a collective gasp. Jesse appears frustrated by the ventilator attached to his mouth, his hands slightly raised as if he is attempting to remove it.

"Okay, I'll ask only Jesse's parents to stay in the room while we get him sorted," the doctor tells us, interrupting Jesse's attempt to remove his ventilator. He presses the red button to summon the nurse. June reaches out a hand, and I take it. She squeezes my hand a little tighter than I'd like, but I understand her need to communicate the emotions she's feeling. Todd stands to the side, hands on his head, eyes fixed on his son.

Then, June pulls me into a hug and whispers her thanks. Next, Todd takes my hand in both of his and squeezes, being careful not to crush my bird-like bones.

"We'll never forget this," he tells me. The sincerity in his eyes carries a multitude of emotions, and I recognize every single one of them.

"Please let us know when it's okay to come back and visit Jesse," I say, smiling. "He's become very special to all of us."

"You have my word," Todd says and then leaves us to return to the doctor's side.

We leave the room and decide to head back to Robbie's, where we can adequately process everything that's happened. The car ride is silent.

We pick up Katie from her mother's, and at home, Katie climbs onto my lap in the living room. We start to weigh the reality of Jesse's return to the world of the living.

"This is the greatest thing that's happened to me," Aileen announces, cupping a hot tea. "I'm in shock," and she probably is. I'm not far off myself.

"Auntie, you did it," Robbie says, "both of you. It was the most phenomenal thing I've ever seen."

"It's a first for me, too, dear," I tell them. "I've never brought anyone back from the brink!"

"Do you think he will remember us?" Aileen's question strikes hard. He might forget everything that happened outside his physical form, just as we all forget our past lives, the longer we stay in our new ones.

"I have no experience to draw from to answer that intelligently, Ai," is all I can offer. Katie hands me her brush, and I instinctively comb through her tangled locks.

"It will be interesting to see if we hear from him in the coming days," Robbie says, placing a tea beside me and sipping from his own.

I nod and release a deep hum. "Jesse will have a lot to work through just navigating his return to the physical world. The rehabilitation will be intensive, I'm sure."

"Tomorrow, we should go to the police with the information we have and ask them to reopen the cold case on Carley Reese," Robbie says what we're all thinking.

I pause to think this over. "I wonder if we should wait for Jesse to share his experiences with the police," I suggest. "We don't have a credible source for the information we received, not by their standards, trust me. I've tried working with the police before. Most are closed-minded about the work I do. I would hate to give them any reason *not* to reopen the case."

"I hope Jesse will be prepared to tell his story," Aileen adds. "I hope he will recall everything."

Chapter 47 - Jesse

Ten days out of my coma, and I'm beginning to feel like myself again. But better! I've reconnected with my parents, and they are elated over my progress and how talkative I've become. Conversational, even. I'm also thrilled over this aspect of my recovery. It's given me a new lease on life. I see a future. I plan to return to school to complete my work. I've decided never to conduct experiments of that sort again, which I used to build my dissertation; however, I will still finish it, because I believe it holds value for the psychological community.

About my time spent in my astral body, I remember everything. Sandi, Aileen, Rob, and Jim's second attempt to silence me. It feels like a dream, but I know better. On the tenth day of my wakeful state, I asked my parents to bring Sandi to see me. She was only too happy to accept the invitation.

"I'm grateful for the work you all did to see me through to this end," I tell her, Ai, and Rob as they sit around my bed. "Or ... beginning," I laugh, throat still a bit irritated after 20 months in a coma. "I certainly found the right people."

"I'm glad you found me," Ai says with a nod. "It was tough at first, but having Rob and Sandi support me, there couldn't be a better team."

"I was drawn to your light, Ai. You are a special person. Not only to me but to the world. You are a healer." As I tell her this, I believe it unequivocally.

"Probably why she's studying nursing while working as a PSW," Rob nudges Ai with his shoulder. They seem to be getting closer.

I focus on Rob next. "You're a healer too, Rob," I say, recalling the light he radiated during my time as spirit. It wasn't a beacon like Ai and Sandi's, but it was good. "And your aura is all the colours of the rainbow."

"That's what Katie said," Rob swallows, "My daughter."

"And, Sandi," I turn my head to look at her. She is a beautiful woman, even in her seventies. But then, I no longer see age. Since I returned to the land of the living, I have started to see auras again. They tend to blur features, but each one is as unique as a fingerprint to me. "Sandi, you are an old soul. You have done so much good here. You have performed so many good deeds for so many. You are a gift to a world that needs your heart more than it realizes."

"You're kind to say so, Jesse," she says, stands, leans over my bed, and kisses my forehead. The sensation leaves me feeling invigorated. I shift my hips, and my legs slide over the bedside. I push myself up and land on my feet. Sandi stands before me. I open my arms in a welcoming hug, and she slips her arms around my thin frame, hugging me back.

As we embrace, Aileen and Rob join us. How could I ever have imagined such an outcome? As someone who was once so disconnected from the world, I am now embracing three people who, though complete strangers 15 days ago, have transformed me into who I am today, who saved me. I know our lives will remain connected. The power of friendship, camaraderie, and fellowship now holds great significance for me. Words I once dared not act upon now define me.

We part, and I remember something noteworthy I must remind them of, "And remember," I tell Rob, with a pointed finger and raised eyebrow aimed at him, "Katie's carpet -"

Rob stops me there. "I have someone looking at it tomorrow, Jesse, thank you," we laugh like old friends recalling a fond memory.

After that reunion, we had several more. Two months after I woke up, it was as if the whole country had discovered me. Journalists flooded my bedside. My story became Carly Reese's story. It became the story of the gold medalist. It reopened the cold case, and every hint Jim provided was confirmed. Rings and remains were recovered, and Jim Reese's name was linked to both murders, along with the attempt on my life.

I've had writers, agents, and producers approach me with offers for books, scripts, documentaries, and true crime podcasts. I'm not opposed to these options, but I'm now back in class and focused on finishing what I started. Professor Sanders is excited to have me back and talking, while Professor Klein has confirmed that I am on the spectrum.

It's all good. I remember fondly that I was once a specter, so being on the *spectrum* will be a breeze.

I've learned not to fear death, but more importantly, not to fear life. To experience it fully, not just as an observer. To get involved. To get to know people. To understand their motivations, rather than just their fears. Because people are multi-dimensional, they don't only endure their anxieties or act out of negative experiences. They learn, grow, and can base future decisions on positive outcomes, building from there.

So, that is what I'm going to do: open myself to others and grow as a person. Life is short, and the rug could be pulled out from under me in a flash. I've experienced that and am proud to say I have learned from it. I want to travel and deliver a TED Talk. I want to do everything that has shut me up and made me afraid. I want a thriving practice. I want a relationship. I want children. I want a cat—no, a dog. What I don't want is to only live vicariously through others. I look forward to tasting life, where I have only ever watched others' expressions as they experienced the bitterness and sweetness, truly immersing myself in living those experiences. I want to feel everything.

If what has been proposed—that consciousness is how the universe experiences itself—is true, then I must do better. I want to be part of that. What did Sandi call it? The Akashic record. I want to contribute and have my contributions leave a meaningful impact.

My eyes blur behind tears of joy as I realize this. Life is for the living, after all, and I've been given a second chance.

When death comes for me, I will not regret having built a life of meaning. Will I miss it? I hope so. Will I fight to stay? I know I will. Because if you are not going to miss it, then it was no life at all.

THE BEGINNING

Michael Poeltl

Read an excerpt from Michael Poeltl's *Killing Karma,* described in many four and five-star reviews, as,

The shadows cast ensnare the characters as well as the reader

"A highly gripping tale that builds a believable world full of unexpected twists and turns. An easy-to-read, engrossing whodunit and why is crafted skillfully here."

No Karmic Debt Goes Unpaid

"... he's (Michael Poeltl) written a succession of novels that dive into the dark side of the human psyche, and 'killing Karma' is one of his finest yet."

Wanted more

"I wanted more. Killing Karma is a thought-provoking book that explores the mysteries and unknowns of this world. We are drawn to and connected with certain individuals. Is that because of an unseen connection?"

Twist after twist and ends with a loud bang!

"The story gives you twist after twist and ends with a loud bang. So, you can expect a high-voltage drama with many plot twists and amazing characters... A bang on psychological thriller for book lovers."

From the opening paragraph to the last sentence, I was captivated

"... at times I found myself holding my breath... I recommend "Killing Karma" to any reader who enjoys turning pages."

The Karma Killer

You reap what you sow.

Newton's Law of Universal Gravitation states that every particle in the universe attracts every other particle with a force that is directly proportional to the product of their masses. Karma acts similarly in that your experiences are directly proportional to the experiences you put out in the world. Karma transcends the present. It follows you through lifetimes. It is a natural law, and like gravity, it doesn't cease to exist if you don't believe in it. Gravity keeps your feet on the ground, the moon in orbit, and the planets moving around the sun. Karma shares this omnipotent quality. Karma keeps you honest. It carries out cause and effect in its own time, and what you reap, you will sow.

We live in the present, but it can be a challenging place for many. Karmic debts are continually being discharged in various forms. Some will experience poverty while others have great wealth. Some will be sickly, while others can't seem to catch a cold. Some will offer kindness to those who'd shown them a similar kindness in another life. Some will die at the hands of those they'd wronged in a shared past.

Karma goes both ways. It is a perfect accounting system that none can avoid, and like gravity, it is a constant. It works through people unconsciously participating in its greater plan.

No karmic debt ever goes unpaid, but sometimes it needs a nudge.

Karma has a champion.

Chapter 1

Having never seen action, Peter thought he'd avoid the punishing effects of post-traumatic stress disorder, but in hindsight, as a peacekeeper in a foreign land, that reality shouldn't have been far from his mind.

Stationed in Kandahar Province in August 2021, he and his fellow soldiers were ordered to fall back to the airport, where embassy and military personnel were being evacuated from Afghanistan. The threat Peter was asked to secure was not the encroaching Taliban forces but the citizens who, in fits of despair over their newly won government, begged to be put on planes and evacuated along with the fleeing military personnel and ambassadors who had helped win back their country.

The scene was one of continuous chaos, day and night, for many days. Peter stood watch where only chain-link fencing kept people at bay after bombs crumbled the tall cement walls days before. Pleas from the growing crowds to let their children through tugged at his conscience. Hateful cries against the escaping forces, leaving them to their fates, were soul-crushing. Their voices cracked with anguish under the weight of another Taliban rule. It reminded Peter of the third panel in Hieronymus Bosch's The Garden of Earthly Delights. Chaos. *Hell.* And he had perpetrated that hell for those people: Pointing rifles and shouting for them to step back. All he wanted to do was help them, but he was a soldier put in a position he hadn't imagined. He relied on his training to steady his nerves. In the moment, it worked. It's what happens after that that isn't easily discussed.

Often, children were pushed to the front of the terminals to appeal to the soldiers' sense of morality. Peter had befriended three of them with what little Pashto he knew. He had given them candies and water during the calmer moments. When, on that fateful day, a suicide bomber entered the airport, Peter watched those three children become engulfed in the explosion. Rifles fired by frightened soldiers threw hot lead at the crowd, who were caught up in a focused charge through the terminal and onto the tarmac in a desperate attempt to escape the chaos and board the military aircraft already moving down the runway. Peter, too, fired on the unfortunate masses – his training overriding his better judgment. His vision had narrowed, and the blood in his ears *thumped, thumped, thumped* against his temples as he instinctively backed away from the stampeding horde. The smell of the detonated explosive and the charred flesh of the innocents permeated his senses. He felt sick to his stomach. It was at that moment he experienced real anxiety for the first time.

His magazine emptied into the air, trying to alter the hoard's trajectory, but the people were not deterred. They fell over the dead, and they fell over the living. They clambered for purchase over one another. The screaming filled Peter's awareness, distorting everyone and everything. He watched helplessly as hundreds stormed the airfield and even leaped onto the landing gear. The aircraft did not falter. A line of bodies on the tarmac followed where the great wheels had run them over. Blood ran like a river collecting in a reservoir where the edge of the runway dipped slightly to the right. The scene was grotesque, and again Peter thought of Bosch's absurd painting.

But that was last year, and Peter vows to get better this year. Several months out of the service, he reconnected with his past love of reading and became the store manager of a small but popular bookstore in the Cornerstone Village district of Detroit. He'd chosen a new city a thousand miles removed from his hometown to separate himself from anything that might trigger his PTSD. Peter is something of a recluse. He feels he's lost his knack for developing interpersonal relationships and has trouble trusting people. Besides, who would want to be with a damaged Vet like him? Peter is content, interacting with enough people daily that he is comfortable being alone in the evenings when he is not at the bookstore. He enjoys the occasional conversation featuring reading lists and favorite books, but tries not to go beyond those topics. He never speaks of his time overseas unless it is at one of his veteran-sanctioned counselling sessions. At night, Peter finds himself back in Kandahar, firing his rifle at civilians. Sometimes he is the civilian being fired upon. Sometimes he is the birdman devouring a human leg in the third panel of Bosch's The Garden of Earthly Delights. PTSD haunts his sleep. It shadows him every second of the day, emerging in his most vulnerable moments. The counselling helps, but it doesn't seem like enough. Maybe nothing ever will be.

After a troubling session with Group, Peter makes his way home, where he rents a two-bedroom apartment above the bookstore he manages. It is an excellent pairing for Peter. He often enters the store during his sleepless nights to read some obscure tome until morning. The potent smell of so many books brings him peace and a sense of presence, while reading gives his mind something to focus on. On June 7th, 2022, a young woman enters the bookstore. She seems out of place in Cornerstone Village, but Peter welcomes her patronage. She is lovely, whereas Cornerstone Village is, well, not.

"Hi," the woman looks to be in her mid-to-late twenties, Peter guesses. Maybe two years his junior. Her stoic expression does nothing to complement her tiny features. The high-set, messy bun, which holds her dirty-blonde hair in place, adds a sense of resolve, flattering her conservative outfit. "I'm Clare," she announces. "Hello, Clare," Peter replies with his customary smile that raises the right side of his face. "I'm Peter."

"I'm here for the book," she continues, seemingly uninterested in his name. She reads the confusion on his face. "I'm Clare? Clare Hastings?" Her eyes locked on Peter's, shifting left to his computer screen as if insisting he finds her there.

Peter thinks her pretty in that mousey, bookish way. He concedes the nonverbal signal, nodding and stepping to his right to pull up the order screen. "Miss Hastings, yes, your book is in," Peter bends down to find the package under the counter. The book is titled "The Many Lives of Mr. Jones." "A curious title," he says.

"It's about his past lives." She says curtly, taking the book from Peter. "Is there a receipt?" Peter looks at the screen again and asks, "Would you like that printed or emailed?"

"Printed, please." Peter does so and hands the receipt to Miss Hastings. "Do you have any other books like this on the shelves?" She glances to her left, where four tall, dark wooden racks create five eight-foot aisles filled with books.

"About past lives? No, I don't think we do." Peter has a relationship with all the books in the shop. If he hasn't already read them, he knows what he's ordered. "I've never read a book on that topic. It sounds fascinating."

"You should look it up. There are lots of books on people coming back." The woman stands stock still, the new book flat against her small chest, her arms crossed over it.

"From the dead?" Peter teases, finding it strangely easy to talk to this woman.

"From the – no, no," Peter catches the whisper of a smile play across her painted lips. "Well, in a way, I guess that's an apt description. But not like a *zombie*. You die and then come back as another life."

"Like the soul reanimating and so on."

"Right, exactly like that. I've been mesmerized by the genre for years." Peter hadn't expected Clare to open up like this but is enjoying the sound of her voice, husky but feminine. "So much so that I've participated in past life regression." She notes Peter's confusion and continues. "It's where you're hypnotized and asked to relive some of your past lives. It's utterly intriguing. The regressionist even records your session so you can listen to it again and again."

"Hypnotized? That's – is it easy to be hypnotized?"

"She knew I would be easy to put under on account of my imaginative nature. A creative mind is an accepting one." Clare seems surprised at herself for running on like this, and Peter thinks he experiences a genuine smile from her. "It's used as therapy for some people. They say that the lives you live when regressing somehow assist in your present. I haven't gone so far as to benefit from that angle, but it appears to work based on my research. I suggest it to everyone I meet."

"Does that include me?" Peter asks playfully.

"Of course, we've only just met." Clare moves her hips and tilts her torso slightly in a mock curtsy. "Thank you for ordering the book. I'll certainly be back." She spins on her heels and moves toward the antique glass door.

"Would you give me the number of the, uh, regressionist you used?" The question forms before he can truly process it. "I think I can see myself trying that." Clare turns again, walks back to the counter, lays her book down, and removes a scrap piece of paper from her bag. Peter hands her a pen, and she jots down an email. He notices her perfume's sweet yet subtle scent as she leans in.

"Send her a note. Her name is Theresa Clement. I'm sure she won't remember me, so it will do you no good to mention my name. It won't get you a discount or anything." She retrieves her book and studies Peter's expression, nods, and turns.

"Thanks?" Peter calls after her, and the bells over the door ring as Clare passes through the threshold. Peter's attention falls to the note. Clare's handwriting is pretty and neat. He types the address into his email client. The PTSD has become a nagging issue of late, and he feels at his wits' end with conventional therapy. Perhaps the road less travelled will offer results?

Chapter 2

The moment Theresa let her guard down and gave life a chance was the moment she knew things would start to get better. Trauma breeds purpose, and it was Theresa's traumatic discovery at her family home on Blackburn Street that put her on a path she hadn't envisioned for herself. When regression therapy was offered as an alternative method to counselling, she felt a spark of recognition. It was inexplicable how the mere suggestion comforted her. She immediately took to the process and decided she would become a past life regressionist herself in a moment of uncharacteristic spontaneity. By 2013, she had completed a course in Lafayette, California. She had plenty of money to pursue whatever path she felt compelled to follow. The course modalities included Hypnotherapy, Reiki, Emotional Freedom Technique, and Bilateral Stimulation. These invoked balance, creativity, self-awareness, intuition, and grounding, which quickly accelerated her personal growth. The work and the therapy helped in understanding the guilt she harbored. But it would be a long road to recovery. The training also helped solidify her life path, and Theresa moved back to her parents' home to begin practicing her new career.

By 2018, she had established herself as the premier regression therapist in her community. She had remodelled the 1960s bungalow she'd grown up in and created an office space from her old bedroom. The International Board for Regression Therapy assisted in guiding her on how she should proceed. Tasteful décor, including candles, salt lamps, oil diffusers, singing bowls, and crystals, gave the space a quality that set her and her clients at ease. A comfortable lounge and weighted blankets offered an additional sense of security during the sessions. It wasn't an easy road convincing people that reliving a past life could assist in bringing emotions and memories from the present to head, but the proof - as they say - is in the pudding.

Theresa found her stride, and the people came. Today, she has a steady list of return clients and many one-offs. These often take the form of bachelorette and birthday parties, as if she were offering little more than entertainment. But they also come in as serious queries. A small percentage of these clients become return clients, which is how she maintains the business.

When Peter arrives for his appointment on June 9th, she reads him immediately. A deep well of sadness lies behind his eyes. *Is it guilt?* She knows that look all too well. There is something else, though. Something closer to the surface. She feels lonely in his presence. He is attractive enough, and just 28 years old, she's noted on the printed form in her hand. Theresa senses a connection to Peter that goes beyond his pain. She will have to meditate on this.

"Hello, Peter," she receives him with a short bow, "please take a seat." Peter bows awkwardly, and she smiles serenely at this. He thanks her and sits on the plush fabric couch beside the door, hands folded on his lap. She notes his discomfort and smiles brightly at him, sitting in the high-backed chair opposite.

"I – uh, thank you for seeing me; I'm new to this." Peter offers nervously.

"Most are, Peter; you don't need to feel uncomfortable with me. I'm not reading your mind or anything," she laughs, and he allows himself a nervous chortle. "What brings you to see me today?"

"Well, I guess my PTSD. From the – uh, Afghanistan."

"Okay, and nothing has changed for you since you filled out the online form? It's the PTSD you want to address with therapy, then?" The question is more of a statement, and she notes the confirmation with a check mark on the printout. "I can tell you I've performed several regression sessions for this very condition," Theresa explains, quietly acknowledging her struggle with PTSD. Though she will not share her experience with him, she certainly empathizes.

"That's reassuring," Peter admits. "It's been a real issue - getting back into a normal routine. A normal life."

"It's a brave thing to accept new therapies or any at all. You've made a decisive step just coming to this consultation." Theresa celebrates Peter's choice to encourage him further. "You mentioned on the form that you've been in Group counselling and attended several one-on-one sessions with psychiatrists. You must have gained some powerful and necessary skills to cope?"

Peter nods yes. "It's been a long road, but I have some tools to get me past certain triggers. Still, it feels as if I'm constantly fighting back the memories. I wonder if I'm going through this for a reason. To overcome some deeper issues. Does that make sense?"

Theresa sits back and nods at Peter, maintaining eye contact. "That's very astute. In my practice, I bring your forgotten past to the forefront to assist in dealing with your present."

"My past lives," Peter says somewhat sarcastically. "I'm sorry, I didn't mean it like that. I'm still trying to get my head around it. I'm not a religious person."

"Then this may resonate with you all the more," she explains. "Regression into a past life is asking a lot of a person experiencing this life. The present is all about what we can see and smell and feel, you know? But in my experience, we've all been here before, and our consciousness has inhabited bodies and lived and learned. It's from past lessons that we can address your PTSD in this life."

"It's certainly a fascinating concept," Peter admits. Theresa notices how he wrings his hands, and she reaches across the coffee table, placing a hand atop his. The wringing stops, and Peter looks up at her. "A habit I developed over the last year." His hands release, and his palms slide over his thighs. Theresa slowly sinks back into her chair. "I've had other strange tics I've managed to overcome, but this one," he pauses, clearly embarrassed, "this one seems to have taken up residency. My hands are so smooth now," he laughs at himself, showing her his palms. "it's kind of ridiculous. I feel like I'm exfoliating myself to death."

"The wringing of hands is a practice of the guilty, Peter. You're not guilty of anything." Theresa uses this to draw out more information on the origins of his PTSD.

"Aren't I?" He looks up at her again and unconsciously returns to the activity. "I kept people from boarding those planes in Kandahar. The bomber and resulting stampede were a result of that."

"I remember seeing that in the news. I'm sorry you feel responsible, but if I recall, you were also protecting others as they boarded those planes to return home."

Peter's expression hardens. "Yes, but the carnage that followed, and for what? Why were we there at all? Spent billions of dollars and so many lives to replace the Taliban with the Taliban. Makes no sense."

"I appreciate what you're saying, Peter, and it's important that you are self-aware of the root cause of your PTSD in the present. It will make choosing the lives you'll face in regression that much easier." Theresa scribbles some notes and returns her attention to Peter. "I'd like to get started as soon as possible. Are you able to come tomorrow anytime between three and seven?"

Peter releases a shaky breath. "I'll be closing the shop at 5:30 tomorrow, so six would work."

"That gives us time then. I'll block off the seven o'clock, and we'll work until we're satisfied with your progress. You may want to clear your evening."

"Will it take that long?"

"I don't like to put a time limit on initial sessions. I want you to find your peace as the trance induction can take up to 45 minutes, depending on the person, and then I can better assess timelines moving forward."

"I'm a little terrified over what we'll discover," he admits, studying his hands.

"Don't think of it like that. It's a healing process. Whatever we discover is designed to assist in overcoming your PTSD. It helps a person return to a trauma to understand the impact that trauma may be having on their current life or behaviors. Current issues may have their origins in a past life, and so in bringing them forth, we heal. It can be difficult, but I believe that hypnotic regression into your past lives is like tapping into an ethereal teacher, but that teacher is you. It's your spirit."

Peter lets out a sigh, "Wow, you really believe in what you do."

"I do, and you'll believe it too." Theresa stands to encourage Peter, who also stands. "Tomorrow then. Six pm." He follows her to the front door, and she opens it for him. He nods and exits her parents' home.

Theresa considers the conversation and notices she has begun to wring her hands. She releases them immediately, straightens her skirt, and thinks, *We're all guilty of something.*

Chapter 3

It was a tough case that ended badly, Harlow recounts. It's the one that got away and has plagued his confidence with every new case he takes on. That was 11 years ago, but the self-doubt has never left him. Having made detective just months before the killings, he approached the scene with youthful ignorance. Sure, he had the training, but this would be his first lead investigation into a double murder. The reporters were chomping at the bit to sensationalize it and at his throat 24/7. His captain at the time had urged him to keep his focus on the investigation and not let anything slip as he fielded questions at the scene.

"Reporters can be ruthless and entitled, Harlow," he'd offered. "Give them nothing they can use to scare the perp into hiding. You've been briefed on this. Just the basic facts. Any evidence, no matter how impressive, cannot be released to the general public."

It was good advice, he remembered, but also a warning. *Don't fuck this up.* The crime was violent and bloody. The residence was in shambles as the perps had ransacked the house for whatever valuables presented themselves. It seemed a classic junkie hit at first sight. Disorganized. Rushed. Probably the murders weren't planned. The couple's lifeless bodies resulted from the murderous home invasion in 2011. Just a couple of meth-heads feeling the pull of their addictions, trying front doors until one opened. In his experience, they'd push past any perceived obstacles to their next hit with reckless violence.

Signs of a struggle were everywhere. The broken glass dining table, the lamp, the skin recovered from under the female's fingernails, and the classic defense bruising on both victims' forearms. Eventually, they succumbed to the perp's beatings and hemorrhaged from head trauma not two feet apart on the carpeted dining room floor.

The ensuing investigation gave up one perp's DNA and the fingerprints of both. Neither turned up in the system, so Harlow had little to run with. As the middle-class neighborhood was canvased, others recalled their motion-sensor lights turning on. Some recounted sounds at their doors and windows that night, but no one had a security camera to identify the perps. It was a frustrating start to a brutal crime, and the newspapers were beginning to develop their own hypothesis. It was an embarrassment that stretched on for weeks.

It did end, however, not with an arrest, but with another double murder. When the newly deceased were fingerprinted, Harlow realized his case was closed. Two tweekers were found in an alley in one of Detroit's less affluent neighborhoods. It was a curious scene. Both were bludgeoned to death, needles dangling from their arms. Would he open an investigation into these two murders? Who would care? The city was satisfied to know the murderers were dead. Was it a vigilante who sought out the Clements' murderers? That never went over well at the station. So, Harlow chalked it up as a failure with a satisfactory outcome.

His failure was felt strongest when he delivered the news to the couple's surviving teenager. She breathed a visible sigh of relief over the deaths of her parents' killers, but he felt compelled to ask her about her whereabouts the night before. She offered a curt response that checked out. She berated him for the insinuation and slammed the door in his face, but not before scolding him for the time it took to find those responsible and then having the audacity to accuse her. The victim's daughter was as disappointed in him as he had been in himself.

Still, he was credited as the lead investigator in a closed case. That never sat well with him, but he wouldn't contest it. He acknowledged the honor and moved forward with his career, one that had flourished under the tutelage of his captain and through the work he put into ensuring that no other case ended the way that one had.

Presently, Harlow is content that Detroit has accepted him as one homicide after another is solved through diligent investigative work backed by years of experience. He is a well-decorated detective who has seen it all. At least, that was his assumption until the calling card of a potential serial killer surfaced.

Pick up **Killing Karma** today for your Kindle or Kobo.

Michael Poeltl

Other Books of Fiction by Michael Poeltl

The Judas Syndrome
Rebirth (Book 2 of The Judas Syndrome)
Revelation (Book 3 of The Judas Syndrome)
Her Past's Present
Waning Metaphorically (14 Short Stories)
\A.I. Insurrection - The General's War
A.I. Insurrection - Armageddon (Book 2 of the A.I. Series)
A.I. Insurrection - Exodus (Book 3 of the A.I. Series)
The Blind Affect
Killing Karma
Cleo McCarthy Time Travel & Other Impossible Things

Young Reader Picture Books

West of Noreso
An Angry Earth

Educational Books by Michael Poeltl

If a Tree Falls in the Forest...
Energy is Forever, and so are YOU!

About the author

Amazon Author Page: Michael Poeltl Amazon
Facebook Page: Michael.Poeltl.Author
Goodreads Author Page: Goodreads
X: @mpoeltlauthor
Instagram: mpoeltl.author
Further Acknowledgements

To whomever, or whatever is seeding my brain with these tales, narratives, and oddities: Gratitude.

Reviews and requests for interviews and guest blogs are always appreciated!

www.ingramcontent.com/pod-product-compliance
Lightning Source LLC
Chambersburg PA
CBHW020058180626
46812CB00006B/2382